PINK MOON

AN OREJ ZANS NOVELLA

SUKALIA BROWN

BLUE POINT PRESS

Blue Point Press
Atlanta, GA, USA

ISBN: PB: 979-8-9877148-2-9

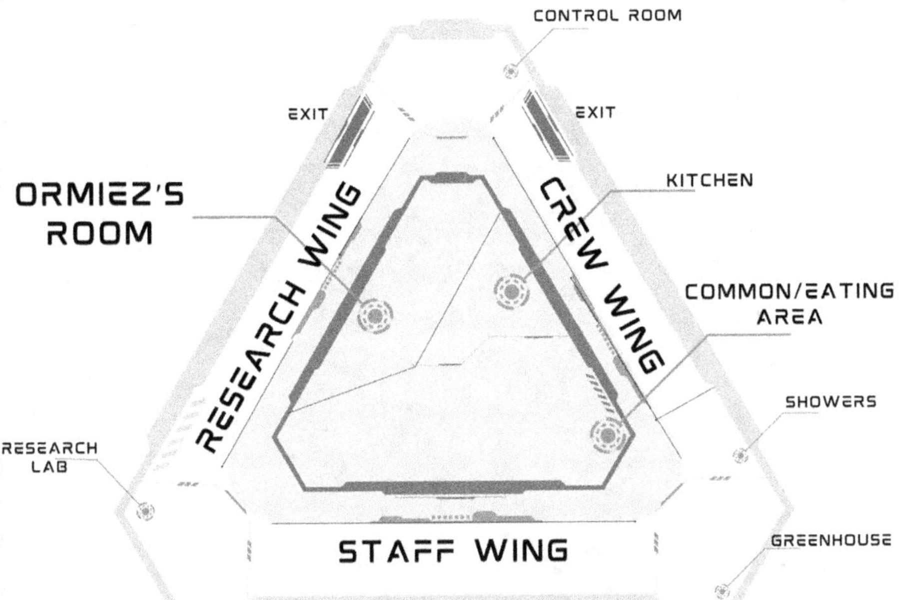

CONTROL ROOM
EXIT
EXIT
KITCHEN
ORMIEZ'S
ROOM
RESEARCH WING
CREW WING
COMMON/EATING
AREA
SHOWERS
RESEARCH
LAB
GREENHOUSE
STAFF WING

1

———

"Who's blood is this?"

And why was there so much of it? Ninety-four slender glass tubes, filled over the halfway mark with blood, sat on the top row of the icebox, a solid chunk of plasma at the bottom of each. On the second row, below the almost pint of blood, was my lunch.

"It's mine, Reg. We had to make space in the temp chambers for the samples." Amaranth said.

He and two other researchers were sitting at the high table behind me, enjoying their lunch. The woman next to him leaned down to say something to another woman, who was sitting on the small sofa next to them. There was every kind of seat in the ship's common area: sofas, chairs, bean-shaped recliners. Stools were bolted to the glossy white floor beneath high and low tables and benches faced the floor to ceiling nature scenes on the left wall. Everyone had their pick of comfortable seats, and nearly all of them were occupied. I guess I wasn't the only one getting a meal in before we landed and went on the first sample gathering excursion.

Even if we got all the samples we needed in one trip, it would still take about nine Okew hours to make it to the site and back, so we needed the energy. I was going to have to eat fast and try not to think about stranger blood sloshing around above my my food.

I grabbed my container, glancing at the five other doors next to the one I held open. There was probably blood in all of them. I sighed and went around to the other side of the meal prep station to warm my rice and beans.

The prep station was a wall that stood at the front end of the common area before the doors leading out to the corridor. Iceboxes were on one side and the heating compartments were on the other. I pulled the clear lid off my container and brought it up to eye level. I read somewhere before that glass food containers were better at keeping out contamination than other materials. *Or was it they caused less contamination?*

I frowned and shoved my food into the empty glass cubby above the sink. The heating compartments ran across the center of the prep station in two rows of eight. As I tapped the blue numbers in the top right corner- adding an extra minute and a half to kill any lingering germs- I focused on the excursion. I was only taking four other researchers with me to the tunnels this first trip. We might not even go in the water, just check the structural integrity of the outside and see if there is enough room for all of us to go down.

Through the blue tint of my food being nuked, I looked out at my crew. All the researchers had gotten into gear already. White diving suits dotted the room, next to dark blue staff uniforms and the beige ones of the ship crew. There were less of the last one, since most of them were working to get us on the ground.

"You think you're talking to one of your nerdy friends?"

The question came from the other side of the wall, right in front of where I was standing. It was whispered, but whoever was talking may as well have said it at regular volume, based on how quiet everyone got after.

"What? No," Amaranth responded. I recognized his voice because I'd just heard it.

"No, *Sijomal*. I briefed you on official rankings and proper etiquette around His Highness before you agreed to come on this mission. You are not to speak in his presence unless directly addressed by the king, and when you are given permission to respond, it is 'Yes, My King' or 'Yes, Your Highness'. Do you understand?"

"Yes, Sijomal," Amaranth forced the words out through clenched teeth.

The Sijomal turned with a look of frustration and locked eyes with me, standing to the right of the prep station where I'd moved unconsciously. The room was uncomfortably quiet, and I got the sense that everyone was intentionally avoiding making eye contact with me. This wasn't the first time I got this vibe from the crew, and now I knew why.

The Sijomal took a second to adjust his face before bowing. "Your Highness, I can have the kitchen prepare another lunch for you if you'd like. They'll have it ready before we land."

Yeah, and the beans would taste like the inside of a can. The kitchen staff assigned to the crew (i.e., me) were good when it came to inner kingdom dishes, but traditional Perjoux dishes, the stuff I'd grown up on, were a challenge for them.

"This is fine," I said, tapping the rim of the container with my fork.

Out of the corner of my eye, I noticed Amaranth shifting from one foot to the other, like he had to use the bathroom. He hadn't moved, besides getting down from his stool, since I came back in. In fact, no one had moved, not even to eat, but I could feel the collective sentiment of 'someone yell fire so I can get out of here' hanging in the air like a thought bubble.

Before I could even turn to him, Amaranth's gaze dropped to the empty bowl in his hand. I was blocking the right exit, and the Sijomal stood between the prep station and high table, essentially blocking the other way, too. Amaranth looked like he was debating if getting out of here was worth the embarrassment of having to ask for permission to speak. If you asked me, it wasn't. I took mercy on him and headed back around the station to the doors. I could eat in my room.

Unfortunately, the Sijomal followed me out of the eating lounge, and ingrained habit forced my feet to slow down so he could catch up to my side. He was a tall man- 5 'ɪɪ, maybe, to my 5' 9- with wide, doe eyes and coily, black and gray hair that grew unevenly all over his face and head.

"What can I do for you, Sijomal?"

"With respect, my king, you don't have to use my title."

"That's not what you told Amaranth."

His brown skin flushed at being called out. "Yes. Those who are so far beneath us in ranking must show honor by using our titles."

Which Amaranth was doing by calling me Regalian, or Reg, *my* title as lead researcher on this project. But the Sijomal didn't care about how we scientists, or *nerdy friends* as he put it, spoke to one another.

Like most people, he probably didn't understand why I wanted to do this mission in the first place. I was one of The Gifted. I received my powers and my crown four months ago. Since then, I hadn't set foot in a lab or done anything relating to research, but I was ready for this. I was ready to be around people who shared my interests and talk about things I actually knew something about.

The scientist in me had been dying a slow death these past months, replaced by a yes man whose only questions were, 'What is this for?' and 'Where do I sign?'.

This research was my chance to feel like me again. Curing food allergies wasn't as important as ruling a kingdom, and people would only remember the things I did with The Gift because magic made everything more interesting, but I refused to drop it. The Kingdom Council could send as many annoying sijomals as they wanted.

"Okay. What can I do for you, Elmer?"

"Elmo, Your Highness."

I nodded.

"I need to go over the ambit with you before the excursion."

Of course. The Council loved their ambits. If this one were anything like their usual, it'd take me the rest of the trip to cut through all the passive-aggressive 'we are your honored servants' bs and figure out what they were demanding me to do this time. I sighed and went back to the eating lounge to throw my food away.

"It's all new policy," Elmo said as soon as I returned to the corridor.

"seeing as we haven't had a traveling king since Xeonere. But we've put every precaution in place to ensure your safety. If you have a moment, I'd like to go over it now."

I nodded again, and he tapped his wristband, pulling up the thumbprint authentication. It was a faveolate screen with thirty-two hexagons attached to one another, one for each person authorized to view this ambit. Only one of them was still lit, meaning I was the last to see it. I pressed my finger to the yellow hexagon and waited until it went dim, then I brought my finger to my temple.

The ambit appeared in the space before me, clear as ever, but to anyone else, it looked like I was frowning at the wall. I scrolled down, skipping over the wordy intro and recap of my mission.

One sentence jumped out at me:

Okew Kings and Queens are prohibited from venturing to or on planets that have not been surveyed and deemed habitable by The Travel Committee.

"What's a travel committee?" I asked, although I could probably guess.

"It's a newly formed organization that will oversee future exploration. Space travel is in our blood, so it's no surprise that you've caught the bug." He smiled. "If more people decide to follow in your footsteps, The Travel Committee will be in charge of training them beforehand. We could have explorers ready in the next few years if you wanted to do another trip. They'd come to the planet first to make sure it's safe, and there aren't any obstacles that might interfere with your mission."

Obstacles. Safe. Vague, catch-all terms that The Council used when they were trying to maximize their control.

"So what does that mean for this mission?"

"Well, since we don't have a committee-trained explorer onboard to inspect this planet, the research crew will stand in as substitutes."

Substitutes sounded a lot like sacrifices when he put it like that. I wasn't worried about anything happening to them. We were heading to an empty planet, and I'd created all the equipment myself. Every face mask, recovery suit, and underwater jet was reinforced with god-given magic, but I didn't feel right sending people out like pawns to collect samples for my research. "I want to go with them."

Elmo's closer smile dropped a few notches. He stood taller and fiddled with the top button on his dark blue suit jacket before clearing his throat. "If you scroll down a few sections, you'll see the stipulation for untrained personnel going on uncharted territory. It's non-negotiable."

I put my finger back to my temple and dragged it down until I found the part of the policy he was talking about.

Non-committee-trained persons may only explore foreign territory with the assistance of an expedited healer.

Fᴜᴄᴋ Eʟᴍᴏ.

And fuck The Council.

My team had gone on the excursion without me, and they came back with enough samples to fill all four of our greenhouse temperature chambers. It was a long trip back to Okew, and everybody was ready to get going, but there was one hold up.

Me.

I was in the seating area of my loft room, pacing and cursing myself for letting The Council see through me so easily. My communicator had pinged over an hour ago with an incoming message from someone at The Travel Committee. It simply said *Planet CDZV is clear for leisure exploration.*

That's what they considered my research, 'leisure exploration', which should bother me. I should be pissed off that I was taking orders from someone I had never met and that The Council had formed a whole division in my kingdom without even asking me. All of that should and did bother me, but what had me ready to turn this ship around and book it back to Okew just so I could tell each of the sijomals to their faces to kiss my ass was the caveat they'd thrown in. If I even set foot in foreign territory, I had to have a bolkin with me. And to my surprise, there was one already on the ship. Meaning they'd been planning to spring this on me from the start. If I gave in now, there'd be a parasite attached to me at all times. I wasn't having it.

I found Elmo in the ship's control room, being briefed by the commander on our return route. "Can I have a word with you, Elmo?"

He turned to me and smiled. "Of course, Your Highness."

The commander was young for a commander, especially one assigned to a royal mission, but he was a highly intelligent man who never needed to be told things twice. He took one look at me, then bowed and turned to one of the many screens that were at the front of the narrow control room.

"I'm going to the site," I said, cutting right to the chase. "Since the team has already gathered the samples, it shouldn't take long for me to get back. We can leave immediately after."

"Okay," Elmo nodded and raised his hand to wave down someone, presumably whoever was in charge of the bolkin.

"I'm going alone."

Elmo froze, then slowly lowered his arm. He leaned towards me and whispered, the same way he'd done with Amaranth in the common area, but with much less animosity this time. "With all due respect, The Council has set rules against that. It was in the ambit."

"That I have not signed or agreed to. In the future, any regulations or committees that The Council wants to establish in my kingdom will need to be run by me first. And I'll need at least a day to consider it." The room was full of ship crew members preparing for take-off, so I said the next part loud enough for them to hear. "I'm portaling down to the site instead of swimming, so that should save time on our departure."

Elmo opened his mouth to give another Council-approved response, but I was done discussing it. I brought my fingers together in the shape of a diamond and mentally summoned my gift.

Creation and destruction. The ability to build and destroy with the same gesture. That was the terrifying thing that coursed through my blood now, binding itself to my genetic material. I never knew what signaled one or the other. How did it know if I wanted to create a tool or a weapon?

People would tell you it's based on character, that a violent person would always use what they created for destruction. It didn't matter if it was a piece of cotton. This was why The Kingdom Council insisted on The Gifted being the rulers of Okew. They believed that Kani would not give his power to someone who wasn't deserving of it.

It was probably also why The Council existed- in case he did.

As the portal took shape in my hands, the planet's black waters filled it, rippling with subterranean currents. I forced it deeper into the blackness, following the route I would have taken had I gone with my team earlier. They'd put biodegradable glow lights along the route to the cave to guide them back out, so all I needed to do was find their trail. After a while of wandering in the dark, I closed the portal and immediately opened another one, this time in a different tunnel. I flattened my palm, going deep into the water until the portal's darkness shifted. The glow light was no bigger than a thumbprint, and because it was the first one in the trail, it had already started to break down, but at least I knew I was on the right track. The network of tunnels beneath the planet's surface was deep and complicated. It could take hours to make it through just one. I got through in three minutes. The trail ended just before the tunnel let out into a larger body of water. I broke the connection between my hands, allowing the portal to widen and drift down a little before stepping forward into it.

My suit had already started lowering my body temperature on the ship, so the freezing water wasn't as much of a shock to my senses, but it was still cold as shit. I swam forward until the oversized rocks of the cave floor started to slope upward. The water was brighter outside the tunnels, more blue than black. I followed that brightness until I broke the surface.

The cavern was a small pocket, no bigger than my room on the ship, that had formed out of stone. Water covered most of the floor, and the roof of the cave was low enough for me to touch if I stood on one of the tall rocks that jutted out of the water. That must have been what the others did, I thought, looking up at the numerous empty shells hanging from the ceiling. Chirorodziva plants could grow with little to no light, which explained why we'd found it here, thriving underground on a planet where nothing else seemed to grow. They always grew behind or under something else, which was a crazy survival advantage when you thought about it. What other lifeform got to look into its own future, decide where it wanted to grow, and what was going to protect it from threats while it did? The shell at the root of each Chirorodziva was an added layer of protection, and it provided nutrients to the plant. I'd asked the team to be as careful as possible cutting down the plants. Just because this planet didn't have a single living thing on it didn't mean it was okay for us to destroy their plant life.

I swam over to one of the three large protruding rocks that were like tiny islands cropping out of the water. This one was wider and flatter than the other two. I turned onto my back and rested my head against the edge, breathing in the freshwater scent of the cave.

Months of preparation and weeks spent on a crowded ship, but, finally, I had made it.

Something about being here made me think of home. Not the palace in Dewar, my childhood home near the moor. I hadn't been back there in years, not since my mom passed away, but I thought about it every day. Until now, I hadn't had a huge urge to go back.

Water splashed against my chin, and a bit of it got in my mouth. It was cold and pretty good until I remembered it was cave water, and I shouldn't be drinking it.

There must've been another inlet besides the tunnels- a big one- because the water level was rising fast, and waves had started to form on the right side of the cave. The flat rock I'd rested my head on minutes ago was gone, under about a ton of water, and soon I could reach out and graze the Chirorodziva shells while floating on my back. The roof of the cave was getting close, and soon I'd have to go under or portal back to the ship.

My diving suit was equipped with everything from body temperature regulation to storage vessels that pulled air from bubbles in the water, so I wasn't worried about having to examine the cave underwater, but I did wonder where it all was coming from.

I tilted my head back to put on my face mask. As I adjusted my breathing, the intuit fiber of the mask molded to my cheeks and forehead. Its white lights kicked in instantly, lighting up my face and more of the cave ceiling. Just as I was getting ready to dive under, a wall of water rose to my right. It happened so fast that I wasn't able to brace for it. The wave crashed over my head and sent me tumbling through the water. I regained control just in time to avoid slamming into a cluster of jagged rocks, but not in time to dodge the second wave. This one was stronger. My body twisted like a solo noodle in the water.

I reached out blindly, trying to find a rock, or wall or, hell, even the ceiling to steady myself, but nothing seemed to be around but more water. My daddy took me diving a lot as a kid, but the way this was going, you'd think it was my first time in deep water.

"Diver's instincts are like muscle memory," he'd always say. "If you get in trouble out there, I'll be there to help, but you need to establish your own routine, some kind of ritual to quiet your mind. You'll know what to do then."

I tried to use my ritual. Instead of the cold cave, I pictured myself back in the warm, familiar waters of Perjoux. I relaxed my body the same way I would if I was swimming on a windy day and let the current drag me down. The waves were less intense beneath the surface. It gave me the space I needed to think. Portaling back to the ship was out- I didn't have the right mindset or sense of location for that- but if I could find the inlet, I could make a temporary seal and stop the tide. It had to be near the bottom since the water was steadily rising, but I didn't hear any pouring in.

My suit tightened against my body as I swam down, fighting against the tunnel currents that pushed and pulled me in every direction. I probably looked like a strobe light that someone had tossed in the water. The diving suits had propulsion valves at the knees. If I twisted the gray caps open, air would shoot from the valves on the side of my shoes and give me the boost I needed to cut through the currents. Any other time, this would've been a last resort because I also needed that air to breathe, but I was also out of ideas.

I opened the valves and jerked forward as bubbles sprayed around my feet. Propulsion valves weren't like jets. They weren't going to send you blasting through the water at top speed, but they were helpful if you found yourself in a situation like I was.

When I got to the slope that led to the tunnels, I closed the valves. The trip back down had definitely been harder than the one up. The pressure had increased so much from the water that my arms and chest felt like sauce packets being squeezed for everything they had. I pulled at the stretchy fabric, turning around in a circle while I searched for the inlet. The light from my face mask suddenly shifted, and a bright red warning flashed before my eyes: AIR INTAKE SEVERELY COMPROMISED.

What? I hadn't used the propellers that much, but as I struggled to pull in my next breath, I realized something was definitely wrong. All of my scanners started flashing then, bright red warnings that blurred before my eyes. Something was squeezing my chest. It got tighter every time I inhaled.

I tried to lift my arm to see the alerts on my wrist scanner better, but a sharp pain tore through me. It cut into my chest like a drill, aiming straight for my heart. I tugged at my suit and roared, causing my intuit mask to shift and water to spill into the sides. It quickly adjusted and resealed, but I couldn't remember how to get the water back out. The pain was blinding. Excruciating. I gritted my teeth and tried not to scream again as my fucking chest imploded.

Coldness worked its way into my body, up my fingers and toes into my limbs.

When it finally reached my chest and the pressure let up, I exhaled in relief.

2

___

One of the things I loved most about growing up in Perjoux was the Midnight Kisses. They were these gigantic plants with dark blue berries that sweetened when you blew on them. We had a field of Midnight at my old house. It grew from the swamp to my window, so close that a few of the leaves brushed the top of the house. I used to use the stems to track my height. I'd stand with my back against the tallest plant, dig my nail into the thick shoot above my head, and check every week to see if the nail mark had grown. Looking back, I realize there was a flaw in my method, but it made perfect sense when I was a kid.

One day I was out checking my mark when a bolkin stepped out from between the Midnight stalks. I say stepped, but I guess it was more like a slither since they don't have feet. Its slanted black eyes were already fixed on me, staring into me with an expression I couldn't read. That was another problem with them. They didn't have mouths or eyebrows, so it was impossible to tell what mood they were in.

This one was hungry, that much I could tell, because I could almost see through its giant, worm-like body. My daddy told me once that they stay in their cloud form when they're hungry in case they run across something wounded.

I used to think it was cool that they could change their form at will to help a person who might've died otherwise. But standing across from the bolkin that day, its long white ears flattened to its head, I realized that there were scarier things than death. Dad also said they couldn't hurt people- they didn't have arms or teeth or anything- but to always be careful around them. Why would he say that? If they couldn't hurt us, why did we need to be careful around them?

I blinked, and the bolkin disappeared.

I'd been so sidetracked, trying to figure out what dad had been trying to tell me, that I didn't notice it becoming more transparent, shifting fully into its cloud state. The white vapor drifted into the Midnight field, rustling the berry leaves as it went. Instead of trying to figure out where it was going, I raced back to my house and slammed the door. My feet didn't stop moving until I got to my room and checked all the windows to make sure they were locked.

I didn't sleep that night. The sound of the Midnight leaves rustling was too loud, and the mist from the moor was ominously heavy. It lurked outside my window. At any moment, a white tail would materialize and tap on the glass. I just knew it.

The next day, I asked my daddy if we could cut the Midnight Kisses down. He didn't understand why I was all of a sudden volunteering to do yard work, but he wasn't going to turn down a helping hand. We got to work not long before sunset. My height tracker was the first to go.

It was brutal work. The stems were super thick and hard to cut through. Not even ten minutes had passed before I'd sweated through my clothes and was having trouble breathing.

"Why don't you go grab a cold drink from inside. Bring me one, too," Dad said.

"Okay."

I dropped my handsaw and wiped the sweat from my face before heading to the house. That was the last thing I remembered before waking up in the healing center. My mama sat next to me, fighting back tears as she told me about the hole in the right side of my heart.

"We'll get it fixed, Ormi. You're going to be okay."

MAMA WAS CRYING AGAIN. Her tears fell in fat drops on my arm and clung to the hairs there. She must have been at it for a while now because the whole underside of my arm was wet. I opened my eyes so she could see I was okay.

The shell covered ceiling greeted me, bringing me back to the present and where I was: underground, lying on the cave floor.

Everything around me was the same, but different. It was still chilly, and the walls were still slick from the water, but now I was lying on the large flat rock in the center of the cave, and there was light- a lot of it. Not the glow lights the research team had left behind, but small strands of pink and blue light that drifted like sound waves above me. I sat up slowly but froze when the light pulled back- like it was giving me space. I rocked to the left, squinting as it mirrored my movement. *So, Elmo sent the bolkin anyway.* This one was different, at least. I didn't think they came in any other colors but white and- when they were feeding- red.

"I'm telling you now. You feed on me, I'm turning you into an air freshener and putting you in the crew bathroom," I said, getting up to my knees.

The dull ache in my chest was a second reminder of what had happened, and this one had me nervous. Diving had never agitated my heart condition before, but obviously, I'd underestimated this planet's pressure. It was a good thing I was alone. Having heart spasms and nearly drowning would not help my case with The Council. Speaking of which, I needed to get back. There was no telling how long I was out. A search party was probably already halfway through the tunnels if the bolkin was here. Couldn't let them see me all laid out.

I stood up and shook the stiffness from my limbs. My feet were tingly inside my flippers, and my hands shook as I brought them together. Like a puddle of water, my power poured into the center of my hands, reflecting the magenta and blue strands of the bolkin's strange light. It was interesting, almost nice looking, but I still didn't want it anywhere near me. Unfortunately, I had already started forming the portal, so I couldn't wave it away. It hovered closely on my right side, nearly touching my shoulder and peering down at my portal, which had gone still. Normally a brewing cauldron of power, it was now a smooth, mirrored surface. I looked down at my reflection and almost didn't recognize myself. My skin was so washed out I couldn't even see my freckles, and I wasn't wearing my mask.

I searched the area around the large rock I was on, being careful not to step too close to the edge. Most of the water had filtered out, so now the floor was nothing but slippery, jagged rocks and open tunnels. One wrong move and I was getting carried out of here by my team.

The bolkin moved. In one uniform motion, all the neon strands of its cloud shifted, moving back to where the rock connected with the wall of the cave. It swirled in a nonsense pattern for a few seconds before individual pieces broke from the cloud and flowed towards a spot on the floor, two tunnel openings away from me. I guess it was done trying to suck up, which was another thing I had never seen them do. Where had The Council found this thing?

I watched and waited for it to return to its solid form, but the strands twisted in long lines and abruptly turned at other points, making some kind of sculpture.

This wasn't a bolkin. They were small minded creatures whose only goal was to eat. They didn't make art. This realization should have been my cue to get my ass out of this cave, but I couldn't move. I wanted to see the final image. Whatever this was, working hard to create something amazing. I could appreciate that.

The blue strands of light transformed into deep brown skin, and the magenta faded into long, dark hair.

It was a woman, or at least a female, and she was alive.

The light dimmed once it was done making her- or maybe *she* made *it*. I wasn't sure. I was still stuck on the fact that a woman had just appeared out of thin air in front of me. Her face was round, and so was her mouth. She had nice lips. Really nice, actually. They were juicy- just how I like them- and almost too big and sexy for the cute little button nose they were paired with.

Wait. What am I doing?

I was not that guy, the one who could overlook a female being from a whole other species if she had a nice pair of breasts.

Breasts.

She was naked.

The last of the light strands had trickled down into the water, causing the pit where the tunnels were to glow a deep purple and leaving her sitting on her heels with her hands folded in her lap. Naked. The tunnel in front of her highlighted her face and shoulders, but left the rest of her body hidden in the shadows. I had great eyesight, though, and there was no hiding that small waist, those soft curves, or those delicious looking brown nipples.

I promise I'm not that guy.

To prove it, I pulled my eyes back up to her face, which was, honestly, just as sexy as the rest of her, and put my hand to my chest.

"Hello. I'm Ormiez."

"My name is Exia," she responded in a language I hadn't heard since I left Perjoux four months ago.

"You speak Enid?" I asked in the old language.

"Yes."

At least I didn't have to make a translator to communicate with her, but now I was really confused. I squinted above her head at the spot where the lights had been, then at her. "Exia, where are you from? How did you get here?"

Stupid question. I'd just seen the way she got here, but I still couldn't explain *how* it happened, and it was bugging me a little.

"I followed your sol signal."

"My what?"

"Your link to this life. It's how I was able to restore you."

"Restore...me."

It clicked then, and my spirit plummeted. I didn't even realize I had gotten my hopes up when I found out she spoke my language. She was crazy. Why were the gorgeous ones always crazy? To be fair, if this was her home, I was probably the first person she'd seen in a long time, maybe ever. Going your whole life with no one to talk to? A little crazy was excusable.

"Is there anyone else here with you?" I asked, just to confirm what I suspected.

"You were given to me only."

"O-kay." We were getting nowhere fast. Everything I asked, no matter how simple, she responded to with nonsense. Maybe I needed to stick to the basic questions. "Can you tell me how you got here?"

"I told you, I followed—"

"I don't know what that is. And I'm having a hard time following you. Can you start over? From the beginning, please. And explain everything, like you're talking to a child or an idiot."

"Is that why you came down here alone? Because you're an idiot?"

Damn. "I'm not sure how to respond to that. Do you want a cover or something to put on while we talk? You gotta be cold down here."

She eyed my suit and shrugged. "I'm fine, but if you have a garment like you mortals wear, I will take it."

"You mortals?" I laughed. Alright. I knew where this was headed, and even though I knew better, I asked anyway. "What does that make you?"

"I am a guardian of the doquime ima sol."

For someone who grew up speaking Enid, I was having a real hard time keeping up with this discussion. Exia used a lot of outdated terms, stuff I'd never heard, even in the most isolated parts of the outer kingdom, and she had a pronounced accent that I couldn't place. "Doquime- that means sleep, right?"

Her mouth opened slightly, and she looked at me like I truly was an idiot.

"Doquime ima sol- the soul's rest."

"*Death.* You're telling me you're a death god–goddess?"

"Something like that."

"Well, which is it? Are you or are you not a goddess?"

She didn't answer, just continued to stare at me with this pitying look, like I was missing the obvious. Not going to lie; it made me uncomfortable. I didn't believe for one second she was a goddess, but there was something weird going on with her. I wasn't sure yet what it was, but something about her was setting off alarms inside me. They grew louder each second.

Then it hit me.

Her eyes.

The Gifted had glowing eyes. It supposedly came from the essence of Kani, that piece of him that lived within his chosen ones.

Exia's eyes were normal, dark brown, almost black. They pulled you in like a siren, but no power glowed in them. So how had she gotten here? I looked down at the swirling water in the tunnel at my feet. The blue and magenta ripples wove together and twinkled like stardust.

She wasn't alone. There had to be someone else with her.

We were very far from Okew, and our thermal scan hadn't picked up anything when we first landed, but maybe we should have checked for ourselves because, obviously, it had missed the two humans living here.

This planet didn't look like much, but if her partner had the gift of creation, he could literally make this the home of her dreams, perfect to live out their lives in complete anonymity.

I always wondered how Vergil, the original scientist who discovered the Chirorodziva plant, knew it was here. He never stated in his works that he'd traveled, but he gave the exact celestial coordinates for where to find it. I made the connection between Chirorodziva and its ability to mask proteins in food that trigger allergies, but it was all theory. I didn't have the actual plant to test it out. I wasn't sure it even existed. Maybe Vergil had visited here at one time. Maybe he was from here.

Veltargin-L, as he was known before he started going by the shorter version of his name, was around during the ancient times when our people routinely traveled in search of a planet to call home. The time of old kings like Xeonere.

This was amazing! I might have found one of the traveler's descendants, and she wasn't alone.

"Where is your king or queen? The one with eyes like mine." I asked as I created a suit for her like the one I had on. What if they were all naked? Should I accommodate their customs? It could earn me some trust, but I was *not* about to meet another ruler with my boys hanging out. That was where I drew the line.

"I don't answer to a king or queen."

Maybe The Gifted weren't as high up in their society. "But where are the rest of your people? Can I meet them?"

"You would have to be between lives to meet my people."

This again. I didn't have time for this nonsense. I told Elmo we'd leave as soon as I came back. Now I needed to convince someone from her group- someone who wasn't out of their damn mind- to talk with me and maybe meet my people. "Fine. I'll find them on my own. Where's my mask?"

My power should have recovered from whatever hiccup it was having before, but if not, I could still swim through the tunnel. Just as I was considering sticking my arm in the tunnel to search for my mask, pressure slammed into my chest like a mallet. It quickly burrowed in and wrapped around my heart.

My vision went black, and any breath I could have taken was quickly squeezed out of me. I must have blacked out again because visions started flickering before my eyes.

I saw myself in the water, thrashing and clawing at my suit. The vice wrapped around my heart tightened at the same time my illusion hunched over and let out a silent scream. Bubbles exploded around his face- my face- which was twisted in agony.

In that moment, I was both spectator and the tormented. My pain was doubled, and so was my fear. I felt the numbness enter my body just as vision me stopped thrashing. Eventually, my mask dislodged as the temperature of my face dropped lower than that of the water. I watched it sink into the blackness and disappear.

Everything had gone still around him and within me. We weren't breathing. I only noticed it on my end because my chest had stopped rising and falling under my hand. His mouth was open, and no bubbles were coming out.

I couldn't feel the emotions that I should be feeling. It was like I was sleepwalking through a nightmare. Strands of light flickered in the water, and my eyes flew open. I gagged and rolled over, coughing up water into the tunnel opening.

Exia was nearby. She looked me in my eyes as I trembled, gasping on the cave floor.

3

———————

I'm a man of science. Evidence and rational conclusions based on that evidence. This was how you didn't wind up misleading people and being misled. But I'm also the king of Dewar, one of The Gifted, imbued with a power that I'm told is from a god, who I've never seen and have no logical evidence of.

It's been hard enough trying to reconcile this new life of mine that contradicts everything in my old life, and now there was this- her.

Exia pulled the suit I'd created for her over her legs and did a little shimmy as she worked the skintight material over her hips. I watched in a daze, too messed up in the head to remember normal shit like manners. In my defense, she'd just watched me tremble like a newborn in the wilderness without even offering me a pat on the shoulder.

She got the suit, which was pretty heavy, on by herself and, without hesitation, tapped her wrists together. The lights flared to life on the arms, knees, and neck of the suit, indicating the survival mechanism had been engaged.

"The cave will fill up again soon," she said, reaching down in the water and pulling my face mask out. "Your team has already entered the tunnels, but they won't make it here in time. We need to cut them off and head back to the surface."

"We? You're coming?"

I figured she'd leave now that I had come to.

"Yes. I'm required to stay with you."

Everything I'd learned about Exia so far said that she wasn't someone who needed to lie. And if I questioned her and made her prove what she was saying, I probably wouldn't like the way she did it. So if she said I needed to get my ass out of here and she was coming with, I had no choice but to believe her.

I stood up, giving my legs time to regain their strength before sliding one foot forward. The tunnel opening was right in front of me. It was highlighted by a swirl of magenta, in case I missed it.

My hands were clammy inside my gloves, and a bead of sweat was moving down the center of my back like it was on a water slide. I tried to move towards the tunnel opening, but fear stitched itself between the soles of my boots and the ground, keeping me in place.

I couldn't do it.

I'd grown up surrounded by water. Swimming came as naturally to me as walking. Yeah, I'd had a couple of close calls before, especially when I started diving by myself, but nothing compared to this. I had died.

"Transitioning is an intense and sometimes traumatic process. I try to spare mortals from it if I can." Exia's smokey, emotionless voice came from the other side of the tunnel opening, some eight feet away. She had put her face mask on and was eyeing me warily through the glass panel.

"Is that your way of apologizing for making me relive my death? If it is, that's a weak apology."

Instead of answering, she bent down and stuck her hand in the water again. "You can portal to the surface and send someone back for the people in the tunnel. There should be time to make it to them and back out before everything seals."

"Everything seals? *What the fuck is happening?* Is the planet collapsing in on itself? Did I miss a major event while I was out?"

"It's transitioning," Exia responded calmly, which only frustrated me more.

"That doesn't answer my question!" I paused and took a deep breath. "How long do we have before this place *transitions*?"

"It's already started. It has entered the ilgune stage."

"I don't know what that means. Is my team going to die- yes or no?"

"I'm not sure. We are at a nexus. Their lives are dependent on the decisions being made right now."

Fuck. I put my mask up to my face, giving the intuit time to register and mold to my face, then closed my eyes and jumped in the tunnel. The water shifted a moment later when Exia jumped in.

My heart was pounding fast and loud in my ears. I couldn't risk swimming blind, so I forced my eyes open.

Cave darkness was different from regular darkness. Even with the many lights on our suits, I still had to go slow so I didn't slam into the rocky walls of the tunnel. Just another layer of anxiety. Like I needed more. Time was literally against me on this planet. My team was somewhere in this maze of underground tunnels, and I had to find them before my heart ran out of my chest and I died down here for a second time.

Something brushed against my right hand, a brief touch, then whatever it was was gone. I jerked my head from side to side, scanning the water with the light from my face mask, but didn't see anything. Something had definitely touched me.

I tapped the moon icon on my wrist to activate the night vision in my mask. Had I not been so thrown off by The Council excluding me from my own mission, I would have thought of this before. The tunnel flooded with heat signals from millions of tiny fish. They crowded in one spot, swimming back and forth from wall to wall.

Their bodies were shaped like peanuts, I realized as I got closer, and they didn't have eyes, which explained the chaotic swimming.

I let my body go slack and drifted closer. If I surprised them, they'd panic, and I wasn't trying to have a bunch of fish losing it around my face. Where had they come from, anyway? This was supposed to be an *empty planet*, yet I was bumping into naked women and blind fish like I was at a beach in Dewar.

At that very moment, Exia's shoulder nudged mine as she swam ahead. The fish parted, forming a wide space for her to come through.

I guess they don't need eyes to see her.

When I didn't move to follow, she stretched her hand back towards me. The appropriate response would have been to grab her wrist, but for some reason, I grabbed her hand. Palm to palm, my fingers squeezing hers, the whole nine. She didn't adjust the hold or let go once we had made it through the horde.

We passed more fish as we made our way through the tunnel. Some were larger than the peanuts, and others I didn't get a good look at because they quickly swam away from us. From Exia, most likely.

Animals were instinctive creatures. If they were rushing to get away from her, why the hell was I holding her hand? I was giving serious thought to this when she suddenly broke our connection and drifted behind me. The white lights of nearly fifty suits shone in the distance. Elmo hadn't just sent my team to find me; he'd sent the whole crew.

WE EMERGED from the tunnel to complete chaos. What was once a hauntingly still planet now looked like a dragon's lair. Pockets of wildfires burned on the ground, and the lightning storm to end all lightning storms was raging in the smoke-covered sky. Bolts barreled down every millisecond, slamming into the ground with a loud crack.

It was a minefield, and at the center of it was our ship.

Multiple gray structures jutted out from the ground. They were each about three stories tall, shaped like tripods, and perfectly equidistant from one another.

They definitely weren't there when we landed.

Whatever they were made of seemed to be a conduit for the storm. Lightning slammed into the peak of the structures and zipped down the three legs, crashing into the ground and sending balls of flame and debris flying. All the water on this planet was subterranean, so it may as well have been raining fire.

"Your Highness, we can't cross on foot." I recognized the commander's voice, even though his face shield was covered in black soot. He had led the way back to the surface and pulled me out of the tunnel. Now it was up to me to get us back to the ship safely.

The red pillars that one of the researchers said looked like giant hands coming out of the ground to cover the tunnels made sense now. Lightning had probably been carving out the rocks for over a millennium. As it stood, they were the only protection we had from the lightning. They were also an obstacle course between us and the ship.

I knew we didn't have long before one of the bolts struck our shelter, so as soon as I stepped between two parallel pillars out into the open, I threw my hands out and forced my power forward. The portal popped open before me so quickly that the commander, who must have been ordered not to leave my side until I was returned safe, stumbled back a step.

Instead of the projection of our ship, there was a mirror image reflecting my team and the apocalypse taking place around us. My power must not have recovered yet from whatever happened to it in the cave. *I can't worry about that now.*

I tilted the portal backward until it was flat on the ground, then turned my palms up, sending it rocketing into the sky. It reached the storm clouds and continued until it stood above the worst of it.

My team gawked at the oval of clear sky and stars that hung suspended like a canopy, surrounded by the swirl of clouds and lightning.

The only person not looking up was Exia. Her eyes were on me, watching me bend nature to my will like a power-drunk god.

It was stupid to be thinking about my pride at a time like this, but I couldn't help it. I needed to show her that that weak, scared man down in the cave was not me. I could survive this and anything else the death gods wanted to throw my way. I'd get every member of my team back to the ship alive, and we'd get there by walking- no shortcuts.

The perimeter of the portal expanded, transitioning from yellow to bright white as I cast more of my power toward the sky until the portal covered a small island's worth of land, including the plateau where the commander had let our ship down. Just for added measure, I created more portals over the wildfires burning in the safe zone. Cold water from the tunnels poured out of the portals, drenching the fires before they sealed shut.

With the fires extinguished and a clear path from us to the ship, I turned to the commander and said, "We can go now."

I didn't let him take the lead this time or wait to see if Exia would follow us. Maybe it was irrational, but I was pissed at her for that shit in the cave. Yes, she saved my life, but then she rubbed my face in it. 'Let's show the mortal how helpless and scared he looked while dying.' She claimed she didn't want to do it, but I knew better. She did it to prove a point, to show me just how powerless I really am. Like I hadn't been hearing some version of this my entire life. Ever since I was a child, people have been telling me how weak I am. Friends couldn't hang out with me anymore because their parents were afraid I'd drop dead in front of them. My parents wouldn't let me out of their sight, even after I'd had the operation to close the hole in my heart. The constant worrying drove them to an early death.

There's got to be some trick to getting The Gift. No way Kani chose him. I'd heard one of the palace groundskeepers say that. Of course, a sickly kid from the outer kingdom wasn't the best choice for a ruler, but I wasn't the one who came up with this stupid method of hierarchy.

And I hadn't complained.

Not once.

I do what I'm told, go where I'm needed, and perform like a fucking magician. I gave up my hobbies, my dreams, and my life for my kingdom. I may not be the strongest or the most dignified king, but at least I care about my people. Even the ones who don't give a shit about me.

"That was impressive," Exia said, popping up next to me. I was so lost in my thoughts that I didn't realize how fast I was walking and that I had left my team, who were still recovering from hours of swimming to rescue me, far behind.

I stopped walking and turned to her. The others were still out of earshot, so now was the perfect time to set a few things straight. "Look, I appreciate what you did for me, which is why I'm not leaving you stranded here. But when we get back to Okew, I want you to disappear out of my kingdom and out of my life. Understand?"

WALKING in my room felt like returning home after a hundred year war. I couldn't wait to get out of my suit and tune everything and everyone out for the next few days, maybe until we landed in Dewar.

I had briefed Elmo and the commander on what happened down in the cave, being as vague as possible in some parts and outright lying through my teeth in others. Of course, they wanted to know what was happening to the planet. Why it was dormant one minute, and the next, we were running our asses off through an apocalypse. With this, at least, I could be fully honest. I didn't know.

I had my suspicions, and they all had to do with one four letter word- Exia.

She'd disappeared when we got back on the ship, dodging the head count and curious crew members who might recognize a new face among them. I wasn't in the mood to explain to everyone that I had drowned and was now repaying the goddess who'd brought me back to life anyway, so she could hide out anywhere, and it'd be fine with me.

Almost anywhere.

"Why are you in my room?"

Exia's eyes narrowed at my tone, but I didn't care.

"I thought you wanted me to avoid the others. You seemed like you were having trouble with all their questions," she said, telegraphing my thoughts back to me. "Or was the problem that you didn't like lying to them?"

She was still in her suit, but her mask and boots were stacked neatly next to a column and a pair of slides I'd kicked off when I was rushing to get ready for the excursion. Her dark hair had dried into soft waves that came to a neat point at the center of her back. Not one strand was out of place despite what we had just gone through. In fact, now that we were safe and in better lighting, I noticed the little things that gave away that she wasn't one of us. Her skin was too even. No scars, acne marks, or even a mole. Face perfectly symmetrical. Posture downright rigid. It was like she was a painting, and the artist was in love with her, so he only remembered the flattering details.

She didn't even get upset when people stared at her too hard, like I was doing. She stared right back from her seated position on the steps that led down to the lazy river in the floor.

When I created this ship, I thought it would be cool to have a river instead of the usual tub or shower. All the walls were projection screens, and mine had still images of Abness Nuk, the swamp near where I'd grown up. It was like bathing in nature. I kept the temperature warm and plenty of plants around to complete the illusion. But now, as I stared down at the shallow river, all I could see was my lifeless body floating in it.

I tore my eyes away from the water and focused instead on finding a flaw in Exia. An eyelash that was longer than the rest, or a booger, maybe. Because nobody spent hours in a tank and came out with a clean nose, not even if they were wearing a face mask. Nothing.

"I guess I wasn't clear. When I said I wanted you out of my life, that included my room."

"Out of your *kingdom* and out of your life," she corrected. "I guess that does include your room, but I can't leave, not until you've completed your W'aminsa."

"Oh, that's all? Well, let's get on that then." I walked around the river and sat on the edge of one of the lounge chairs that doubled as daybeds in my seating area, bracing my elbows on my knees. "First off, what's a W —that thing you said?"

"The W'aminsa is an assignment that tethers you to this realm until you've completed it."

"Interesting. What's the assignment?"

I was being an asshole, but she didn't seem to mind as long as we were coming up with a plan.

She lifted one delicate shoulder before responding. "I don't know. Your W'aminsa was given to you by the other gods."

"Are you talking about The Gift?" I looked down at my gloved hands. "My power?"

"No, but that could be helpful during this."

"Really?" I chuckled. "Because it wasn't much help to me in the cave."

"You were never supposed to be down there in the first place. Powers don't protect you from your own ego."

"*Ego*?" I had to rock back in my seat on that one. "Wow. That is wild coming from you." She had the nerve to furrow her brows like she didn't know what I was talking about. "Your little light show with the water. Destroying the planet with us on it. I know that was you. I get it- you're a goddess, and we *mortals* should tremble at your feet."

Exia said nothing during my rant, but she took one step down into the lazy river. As the ripples fanned out, the color shifted to a deeper green that matched the wall projection perfectly. I hadn't noticed the slight flaw in my creation before, but, of course, she did.

She took one deep breath, like this conversation was just as exhausting and unwanted for her too. "Mortals are ruled by their own understanding. It doesn't matter what I tell you. Until you see it with your own eyes or experience it for yourself, it doesn't exist. You didn't believe I was a goddess until I showed you. And now, you don't believe me about the W'aminsa. You think you were chosen at random, given a second chance for the sake of ruling over some small kingdom on an unremarkable planet. It's inconceivable to you that you were meant for something more. That something as important as a W'aminsa would be assigned to someone like you. Maybe you're right."

She stood up and didn't wait for her feet to dry before crossing the room to the door. "When you're ready to take this seriously, come find me."

She touched the scanner next to the door, the one that only works for my hand. I was the ship's master programmer, so all the scanners automatically worked for me. Everyone else had to be manually connected to the ones they needed access to.

The frosted glass door dematerialized, and Exia strolled out with her shoulders back and head high.

4

———

Headaches were a normal and mildly inconvenient side effect of ship pressure. I was told this the first day of our mission. Since then, I'd had fifteen of these mild inconveniences, but none of them compared to the rampage taking place in my head when I woke up. My mouth was dry, and I felt like I'd been spinning around with weights in my hands. I was also drenched in sweat.

My bedsheets clung to my back as I rolled over and dropped my feet to the floor. I must have been sweating the whole night. I peeled the gray sheets off and took a quick whiff. Just like I thought, they needed soap and water asap.

The dim lights embedded in my room's ceiling flashed twice, signaling someone was outside my door. *Could be Amaranth with the results from the first round of testing.* We all thought it was best to start testing the samples against the blood as soon as we got them, instead of waiting until we got back to Okew. Just in case they didn't last long outside of their natural environment. Corda, the ecologist, and I would work on propagating and sustaining the plants.

It wasn't Amaranth or anyone from the research team at my door. I knew because whoever it was had started banging on the wall. I wasn't your average king. I ate my meals in the common area with everyone, opened up to them about my life before The Gift, and listened to them whenever they had problems. So things were pretty casual with me and the people on the ship, but even they knew better than to come to my room first thing in the morning and try to rush me. So it could only be Elmo on the other side of the door. His position as sijomal gave him more privileges with me than everyone else. Or at least he thought it did.

My guess was confirmed when I heard him yell, "Then break it down! He's in there!"

Footsteps- multiple- echoed in the corridor outside my room as I pressed my hand against the scanner. The door dematerialized, and Elmo looked up from his communicator with wide eyes; then his face went slack. He stared at me for a full minute, blinking like I had just slapped him or something.

"What?" I asked, looking back to see if there was something behind me.

"You're alive," he gasped.

Now it was my turn to stare. "Elmo, you and I are going to have to talk about working hours later, but for right now, I'm just gonna tell you I'm not in a joking mood."

"It's not possible. He wouldn't take it back." Elmo continued to mumble to himself, not hearing any of what I'd just said. He stopped suddenly, and his brows jumped to the middle of his forehead. "You don't know?"

"*Know what*?" That came out harsher than I intended, but my head was still hurting, and my pajama pants were riding uncomfortably because of my sweat-soaked boxers.

He looked down at the diamond-shaped hand device he had been jabbing at when I opened the door and tapped one of the buttons. A white light shot up from the communicator screen and folded open. He hadn't called anyone, so the screen reflected what was in front of it.

My hair was smushed in on the right side and visibly dry. It was time for a haircut. I hadn't had one since we left, and now I was rocking a short afro that could be cool if I cleaned up the sides a bit. My freckles were back to their normal intensity, taking up space on the outer side of my cheeks, and I had gotten my color back. My eyes were the last thing to catch my attention. Eyes had always been the least remarkable thing about a person to me, and I knew what mine looked like. They hadn't changed in thirty years, except for four months ago when they started to glow a bright yellow.

That yellow was gone now, and so were the powers that came with it.

Time slowed down as my dark brown eyes, which had become unfamiliar after all this time, gazed back at me. I registered Elmo closing out the screen and sliding past me into my room, but I also didn't. He was muttering something that almost sounded like a prayer. I had never prayed to Kani or any of the other gods, so I wasn't sure, but if there was ever a time to speak with the higher ups, it was now.

"I need to contact The Council. They'll know what we're dealing with. They have to."

Elmo rubbed his head a lot when he was agitated. I learned this during my first month as king when I'd ask him to repeat himself because I had drifted off or wasn't listening. That habit probably wasn't the reason for his patchy hair, but I'm sure it didn't help.

He gripped a chunk of hair at the back of his neck and gave it a good tug before letting go and doing it again. I didn't believe in signs, but watching my composed sijomal yank his hair out felt like a clear indicator that things were bad.

"What the hell am I going to tell them?"

Scratch that. Now I *knew* we were fucked. I'd never heard Elmo curse before.

"I'll call them," I said. This was my screw-up, so I should be the one to deal with the fallout. "I'll tell everybody on board, too."

"No!" He rushed over to block the door scanner with his body. "They can't know. The Council never announces the passing of The Gift until the next recipient is found and they've had time to train him or her. We don't even know if your gift has passed to anyone else because you're still alive."

I'm still alive.

But I wasn't yesterday.

"You have to stay hidden," Elmo continued, "until I can speak with The Council and get directions on what to do. Most of the ship's functions are still working, and my communicator is connected to the main system back home. It's late in Okew, but someone will answer."

He attacked his hand device, and the call screen came back up.

"*Most* of the ship's functions are working? Not all," I asked.

"No, they went down during the night while we were waiting out the storm to take off. Everything came back up, but it's glitchy, and the fuel supply is decreasing. The commander has shut down the lesser-needed parts of the ship to preserve energy."

"Hello, Elmo." Sijomal Hamp's round face filled the screen. He was an older man- older than Elmo even- with a wide nose and bulging eyes. "And good evening, Your Hi—"

He went still for a second, then leaned forward and squinted at me through the screen. His beady eyes were like a flashlight being waved in my face. I didn't like the immediate accusation that came to them.

"We don't know how it happened or who The Gift has passed to," Elmo said, breaking our stare off. "No one on the ship has seen him yet, so they don't know."

"Good. We'll keep things quiet until we can find the recipient," Sijomal Hamp said. "Are you able to return to Okew in the meantime?"

"No. Our systems are acting up, and the fuel supply isn't enough to sustain us and get us home," Elmo responded.

"Okay. I'll contact The Travel Committee and have a rescue ship sent out immediately."

"Thank you, Sijomal."

Hamp waved his hand dismissively. "No need for that. Sit tight, and I'll get you home. Good night."

"Goodbye, sir."

Sijomal Hamp ended the call without another word to me. Not that it mattered. He'd always been the most critical of my potential as a leader. That first day, he had looked at me with my hundred layers of swamp mud that they were supposed to polish into something that could pass for a king and dropped his head in defeat. So I'm guessing me losing my powers was a surprise to him but not an unwelcome one. Now that I was just another Dewarian again, they could move on and train someone else to be a great ruler. Someone noble and devoted to his kingdom. Not someone who, four months in, would insist on taking a crew into space to search for mythical flowers.

Four months.

Had I known that was all the time I had, I would have put my all into being a better king, the best king Dewar had ever had. I would have helped people and changed their lives for the better. I would have been selfless. Someone they'd be grateful for, even after they found out I was a mistake.

It was past the point of mattering now, but the least I could do was face my crew and let them know they wouldn't be going home right now, and it was my fault.

"Where are you going?" Elmo's voice went up an octave as I approached him and the scanner.

Doing right by everyone included The Sijomal.

I took a step back and rubbed my hand down my face. "What do you think is gonna happen in the next few days when we still haven't taken off and no one's seen me? People are going to want to know what's happening, and the person they're gonna come to for answers is you-unless I explain everything to them now. I know you've never dealt with anything like this before, but trust me, the last thing you want is a bunch of angry *and* confused people on your hands. Confusion causes fear. Fear causes panic. Do you get what I'm saying?"

It took a minute for it to sink in, but eventually, Elmo quietly nodded. We were in survival mode until the rescue ship got here, which meant staving off mass hysteria for as long as possible.

"Have everyone come to the eating lounge," I said, deciding to wash my face and change my clothes before I left. The first rule of maintaining order: remain calm. I was anything but. However, my experience as a plant scientist had taught me that a strong exterior could hide even the greatest weaknesses.

THE EATING LOUNGE was the widest area of the ship and the only place with enough space to hold the entire crew. Servants, kitchen and ship workers, and researchers squeezed into the large common area, shuffling around to find available chairs and stools. Someone flopped down into the curvy lounge seat in front of me and scooted forward, nearly coming into my line of sight. I had my head down, leaning against one side of the prep station, pretending to look at something on my communicator.

At least no one would question why I was sweating so much. I didn't think it was possible, but it had gotten even hotter in the time I'd walked from my room to the meeting. I could already hear people complaining and asking about the heat.

"He's okay?" I overheard the commander ask Elmo, who was standing by the wall projection of Dewar's southern market. He was probably in the group I'd heard running off this morning to find tools to break down my door.

"Y-yes. Yes!"

Smooth, Elmo. He would have been fighting off a mutiny after the third day while Sijomal Hamp called every morning from his desk to congratulate him on following orders.

"Everyone's here," Elmo suddenly whispered in my ear.

I flinched and looked up at him. *How did he get over here so quickly?* He mouthed 'sorry' and took a step back.

"Oh, my *god!*"

The girl sitting in front of me was the first one to notice my eyes and sound the alarm. From there, the room went up like a swarm. Questions flew at me from every direction. People were screaming. Their voices blended together in a tsunami of noise that crashed with enough force to decimate the inner kingdom. One woman was already crying. I focused on her for some reason, watched the tears roll down her face and fall onto the white tabletop. She wasn't saying anything. It was like she had peeked into the future and knew exactly what I was about to tell them.

"Hey! Quiet–" The commander walked to the front of the crowd, fanning his arms up and down in an attempt to calm them. "*Everybody quiet down!*"

The noise continued like he hadn't said a word. Suddenly, a sharp whistle cut through the air from the back of the lounge. I didn't think it would work. People had started standing up and yelling louder to be heard over everyone else. It was going to take more than a whistle to calm them down.

Luckily, I was wrong. The volume in the room decreased as everyone brought their voices down to a disgruntled rumble.

"We all want answers, but we can't hear them if everyone is screaming," the commander yelled. "If you don't feel you can sit through this meeting, leave now, and I'll send someone after to brief you."

Two people got up and left, including the woman who had been silently crying. I wanted to be the one to tell her we had a plan to get them home, that she would not spend the rest of her life on this planet. Hopefully, whoever talked to her later on conveyed it right.

The crowd parted for the people and came back together without a word, and the commander lowered his arms, turning to me with a scowl.

You and everybody else, boss. Alright, let's get on with this.

I cleared my throat and took one deep breath in before speaking. "At some point during the night, I lost The Gift. I'm not sure how or why it happened, and at the moment, we don't know who it has passed to. As you all know, I created this ship, and it is linked to The Gift. At the moment, our fuel supply is declining, and some of the ships' systems are failing. We've already contacted someone back in Okew and they are sending a rescue ship to pick us up. So we have to sit tight until they get here."

Before I could force in another breath, three hands flew in the air. I pointed to a woman in a kitchen crew uniform first. Halle- she was soft spoken, and I had talked to her for an hour one day about her family's embroidery business.

"When will the other ship be here?" she asked.

"Um, it took us a little over three weeks to get here, so we're probably looking at that much time for them, too. At the mo—," *Stop saying at the moment,* "Right now, we don't have an estimated time...but they've already left."

I didn't know if they had left yet or not, but I needed to say something to soften the blow because Halle's eyes had started to tear up when I said three weeks. She didn't respond to my answer, so I took the out and pointed to the next hand: Fred, a man from my research team.

"What do you mean you *lost* The Gift? Are you saying Kani took it back? I didn't know that could happen."

"Yeah, me either. I thought it only passes when someone dies," another researcher said.

"He must have done something," a man in a servant's uniform whispered, but I still heard him. Apparently, Fred did, too.

"Like what? The Gifted do whatever they want, and none of them have ever had their powers taken away."

While they discussed what I could've possibly done to fall out of Kani's favor, I scanned the faces in the crowd, checking to see how the news was being received and if anyone was going to need help processing all this. I locked eyes with Exia four faces in. She was sitting sideways in a chair near the exit. *Enjoying my humiliation?* If it were cake, she'd be licking the plate right now. She'd gotten her hands on a ship crew uniform. The beige one piece, with its herringbone style top and baggy pants, actually looked nice on her. I guess even death gods had a color. Neutral tones were Exia's.

I tore my gaze away from the enigma sitting in the back when another hand went up.

"Yes."

"Do we still have to call you king?"

5

———

I knew she'd be the first to come find me. There was a line of people after the meeting wanting to ask more questions- like I somehow had more answers then- but Exia left as soon as the group questions were over. And now she was waltzing through my doorway without knocking. All the doors on the ship were open now, including mine, just in case the scanners malfunctioned. We didn't want anybody getting trapped in one of the rooms.

"Why is it so dark in here?" her sultry voice drifted over and wrapped around me.

"I thought you'd appreciate the darkness, Death Maiden."

She hummed quietly, like she was considering it. "The blue lights on the ship are irritating to my eyes, but I like seeing what's in front of me just as much as you mortals do."

Despite what she said, she didn't seem to have a problem finding her way in the darkness. She side-stepped the three water canteens on the floor and my rumpled T-shirt with no problem. The wall projections were blank, and all the lights except the emergency one in my lab were off. My bedroom was the largest on the ship and the biggest drain on energy. I'd cut everything off to preserve what we had.

"Are you still upset about the meeting?" she asked out of nowhere.

"Why would I be upset? I'm the one who screwed up."

The light sound of water splashing filled the room as Exia sat down on the ledge of the in-floor river and stuck her feet in the water. She gave me a slow once over from where I sat on the opposite side in nothing but a pair of black shorts. It could be my imagination, but her eyes seemed to linger on my thighs and chest. That was fair since I'd eyed her like she was three course spread down in the cave. Unlike me, she was decent enough to avoid staring directly between my legs.

"You tried to make it right, and all they did was criticize you for it."

Criticize was putting it lightly. We had to cut the group questions short after someone suggested that the researchers were here to study their reaction and that this was all an experiment they didn't sign up for.

"They're just afraid," I said. "Nothing like this has ever happened before, and the higher-ups don't have any answers for them. Can you blame them for feeling like they're being played with?"

"Is that directed at me?"

I shrugged. "Maybe."

Taking one last deep breath, I scooted forward on the ledge. Maybe if I took things slowly this time and gradually worked my way into the water, I could avoid a full-on panic attack. The water was cool against my overheated skin, and even though my heartbeat immediately picked up, I closed my eyes and let out a sigh. This planet's weather had two settings: brain-melting heat from the distant solar flares or lightning showers with a side of rain. The portal I'd covered us with protected the ship from the storms, but it also left us fully exposed to the heat.

"Why are you here, Exia? Not in my room, but here, on this planet still. I know you said you can't leave, but why?"

She eyed me for a minute before responding. "When I revived you, a bond was formed. Our sols are linked now, and as long as you are in this realm, or until you have accomplished what the gods have set for you, I can't leave."

"Wow. So I've trapped you here too?"

"I made the choice to come, but if blaming yourself motivates you to finish the W'aminsa, then yes, this is all your fault. So is the weather."

I snorted. "The weather?"

"Restoring life requires a lot of energy." She dragged her fingers across the top of the water, just enough to send small waves rippling my way. "Some of it has to be borrowed from the surroundings. This planet didn't have much, so I needed to take it back a few phases."

"Take what back? The planet?"

"Yes."

"Wait." I put a hand up. "You're telling me you *reversed time* to bring me back to life?"

"I did what needed to be done. The gods chose you for the W'aminsa. You can't finish it if you're dead."

Well, she was right about one thing: we humans only accept what we can understand. As I tried to wrap my head around everything she was telling me and the sheer amount of power that was in the small woman across from me, I could only think of one thing.

"Why me?"

She looked up from her ripples and scanned my face. Her eyes narrowed as they touched every angle. There was so much in that puzzling stare of hers. It made me want to put everything off to focus on trying to read her mind.

"I don't know yet," she finally answered, "but I am interested to find out. What were you doing when I came in here?"

The subject change brought me back to my current state of panic, and I had to shake my head to remember the answer to her question. *You were recreating your death to find out why they brought you back, but not your powers.* Right. I wasn't about to tell her that, though. Instead, I scooted over the last bit of ledge and lowered myself into the river.

The water sloshed beneath my ribs, with some of it splashing over the brass tiles that lined the edge. I stood completely still with my fists clenched in front of my shorts, not because the water was uncomfortable, but because it was already becoming hard to breathe. Panic attacks either seeped into you or they hit like an asteroid. This one was coming with flames. The twenty minutes I'd spent sitting with my feet in the water had done nothing, so I took a deep breath in and held it.

It might seem counterproductive to hold your breath when you're hyperventilating, but I had learned from past instances that this was the fastest way to get my anxiety under control. Tightness filled my chest, pushing out the quivering nerves as my lungs struggled to take in air. When I couldn't hold it anymore, I released it in one big gust. Tension flowed out of my arms and legs, and my heart raced a couple of seconds more before settling back into its normal pace. Crisis not fully avoided, but at least I was in the water.

I rotated my shoulders to get the last of the stiffness out and turned in time to see Exia shove off the ledge. Her crew uniform got soaked through instantly from the collar down. The fabric nearly matched her skin when it was wet. *Something you shouldn't be noticing or thinking about.* So, I definitely shouldn't be noticing that her nipples were hard or thinking about how they got that way since it wasn't cold on the ship.

She sank lower in the water and stretched her hand out toward me. The first time I held her hand was an accident, but now- just like then- as my palm pressed against hers, it felt natural. All the fear and nerves took a backseat to whatever this magic was she had over human emotions.

I squatted low until I was eye-level with Exia in the water. Her chin bobbed just above the surface, and every time she moved her arm to stay afloat, it would cause water to splash on her chin and those juicy lips. It was damn near erotic, and I couldn't look away if I wanted to.

She pumped her arm again, swimming close enough that I could see her pupils dilate whenever she started to sink. Without thinking, I wrapped my other arm around her waist to steady her.

"The water's too deep over here. You can go back to the stairs. I'm alright now."

She adjusted our grip, twinning her fingers with mine under the water. "No."

I could tell there was no moving her on this. Exia was a little stubborn. The realization, oddly, made her more endearing and human.

"Okay. I'm gonna go under now. If you change your mind, you can let go."

She just looked up at me, waiting. For what, though? Her eyes hadn't left my lips. Did she want me to kiss her? No, she was waiting because I'd just told her I was about to go under the water, and like a parent of a weak swimmer, she was keeping a close watch. Kissing or any other adult activity was probably the furthest thing from her mind, and it needed to be the same for me. With that in mind, I pulled my arm from around Exia's waist and took a breath before sinking down into the water.

This experiment served two purposes. The first was getting me over my newfound fear of standing water. That was coming along, but the second? The one that would hopefully get us off this planet before three weeks was turning up dead in — *Nope. We don't use that saying anymore.* I was having trouble getting it to yield results. But this time, I had Exia here with me. Maybe she was the missing piece.

I closed my eyes and let my mind drift back to the cavern.

It's dark and quiet, and I'm drowning.

Instead of focusing on what was happening to me like I did the first time Exia showed me, I focused on my surroundings. Maybe there was something there that I had missed, something that I was supposed to take with me. But all I could see in my head was black water and bubbles. The lights on my suit offered just enough glow for me to see my silhouette as it thrashed around and the magenta strands of Exia's power as she came to save me.

Why couldn't the gods have been more clear about what they wanted? They could have come to me while I was asleep or as a talking fungus. I mean, I would have thought I was going crazy if a fungus started talking to me out of nowhere, but still, it would have been better than this: semi-drowning myself every day to unlock a hidden memory.

I needed air.

When I resurfaced, Exia raised her brows in question. Right. She didn't know about the experiment I'd been working on for the past two days. No one did. They all probably assumed I was in my room moping over losing my crown.

"I'm trying to figure out what I missed," I said, wiping the water from my face. "Do you have any ideas about what my W'aminsa could be?"

Her mouth formed a little O as she quickly caught on to the premise of the experiment. She closed her mouth and absently gnawed at her lower lip while she thought. I tried not to stare.

"W'aminsa's are usually about sacrifice. The person has to give up something of themselves. Something that's intrinsic to who they are."

"I've already lost my powers and my title. What else is there?"

"Were those things important to you?" She tilted her head to the side, not taking her eyes off me as she waited for my answer.

"*Yes.*" That was obvious, wasn't it? I loved my people. And who wouldn't want to have magical powers? I may not be destroyed over not having to put up with the superior looks from the other royals anymore, but *my powers*? I'd just gotten them.

I did what everyone did during the first few days, created a bunch of shit that I didn't need but always wanted, but then I got serious. It was time for me to start my new life as the king of Dewar. And I had turned myself inside out to do it, working night and day, studying the past rulers and The Gift, figuring out how to be more dignified, make it less obvious that I wasn't brought up in luxury. I didn't curse (out loud) anymore when I was around people. Because kings quoted philosophers and used their voices to inspire greatness and evoke solidarity. They didn't need to resort to base language that even a child could use.

The Council told me how to dress, who to befriend, and how to work my way into their circles. I learned Okrian, a language that's mainly spoken in the inner kingdom because none of the royals spoke Enid.

"Enid is the language of the first king," one of the sijomals told me. "His people- our ancestors- suffered and died for him. We don't speak his language in honor of them."

More likely, they didn't have enough interactions with the Enid-speaking people of the outer kingdom to warrant learning it.

Nevertheless, I did everything they asked, no matter how big or demoralizing. The only place I messed up was when I tried to hang on to a small part of myself- my research. I figured people would appreciate knowing that the man who was randomly chosen to lead them was at least not an idiot. But now, seeing where all this has led and the huge inconvenience it's caused everyone, if I could go back, I'd hand my research off to someone else.

I swam back to the stairs, only letting go of Exia when the water was shallow enough for her to stand up in. She took one step onto the white stone, then paused. Without turning around, she said something that would haunt me for the rest of my time on this planet.

"You lost your powers after everyone was safe on the ship. They could have taken them sooner, as soon as you died. My guess is, that was just to get your attention. Something else is coming."

6

———

"**K**nock knock. You in here, Reg?"

From my bedroom overlooking the first floor, I could only see the top of the person's head who was standing in my doorway, but those black braids with purple ends could only belong to one person. The research team had been quiet since the meeting, but I knew they were just as concerned as everyone else. The difference was they assumed there had to be an answer, and of course, we were missing it because our focus was on overreacting. It had been eight days, according to my body's sleep cycle. Long enough for them to come up with every potential solution and poke holes in it. Now the panic was setting in.

"Yes. Come in, Amaranth."

I rolled out of bed and padded over to the scanner behind my wilted ippa plant to turn the lights on. The lower level lit up, and Amaranth looked over the waist-high railings at me and cringed. He quickly adjusted his expression, even though it wasn't necessary. I knew I looked like shit.

My pants and shirt were wrinkled and had random sweat stains on them. I'd started sleeping fully clothed since we opened the doors because it was guaranteed that at least three people would walk in here every day. Elmo for his 'yes, he's still in his room, and everything is fine' call with Sijomal Hamp, someone from the cook staff to tell me what they would be preparing today and when I could eat it, and Exia for...I don't know why.

She'd stopped helping with my experiment after the fourth attempt. Said it was a waste of time, and she wasn't here to help me punish myself. So now, when she walked in every day, she went straight to the little nook beneath the stairs that lead up to my loft bedroom and sat down on the floor with her legs crossed. She'd stay back there for hours, hidden by the tall, crispy leaves of my plants, and when she'd come out, she'd be different somehow. I couldn't explain it, and I hadn't gotten up the nerve to ask her what she was doing just yet.

"I didn't mean to wake you, Reg. I just wanted to get here before everybody else did to pick out my spot."

"What are you talking about?"

My mind was always a little slow when I first woke up.

"I won the drawing for the research team."

I blinked once. Twice. Nope. Still not making sense.

"What drawing?"

"The one to move in here. Remember the name drawing was after dinner last night?"

It finally clicked what he was saying, like a timer hitting zero. A lid creaked open in my chest, and venom poured into my bloodstream. "I don't remember because I was never told about this."

"Oh," Amaranth said dumbly. He shifted his weight to his left foot and looked at me with an expression that was in between polite and constipated.

"Who else won the drawing," I asked.

"Um, for research, it was me. Halle won for the kitchen crew drawing, and–"

"There were *multiple drawings?!*" *Okay. Calm down. Amaranth obviously didn't know what he was taking part in.*

"Yeah. Every department had a box for people to put their names in if they wanted to be selected. I thought you knew. They said it was your idea. I thought you were trying to ease some of the tension with the crew."

No, but I should have. But also fuck that. Who were they to give away *my* room? "What else has been happening that I don't know about?"

"Well, I don't know what you do or don't know, Reg."

I took a deep breath and swallowed the rage that was building a second time. "Just tell me what people have been saying."

Amaranth made this weird tongue clicking sound before responding, "Some are saying it's going to take longer than three weeks for the rescue ship to get here. Some think they aren't coming at all. They say The Kingdom Council would only expend that much resources for one of The Gifted, which you aren't anymore. And you heard the evil researchers theory in the meeting."

I nodded, processing this. I knew my lie about the rescue timeframe hadn't convinced everyone, but I didn't know they were expecting The Council to leave us for dead. "What do you think?"

He twisted his mouth and shrugged his shoulders. "I got a few conspiracies. They mostly have to do with the woman you brought back with you from the caves."

Fuck. He knew. "What woman?"

"Exia: brown-skinned chick, weird accent, showed up out of the blue around the same time you lost your powers. It can't be a coincidence, right?"

Negotiation was one of the first things The Council worked on with me when I became king. Their advice was to never confirm anything- like ever. If a person knew enough to do damage, your input would only strengthen their ammo. So I really needed to sell this next lie. "Unfortunately, that's exactly what it is, Amaranth, because she didn't just show up. She's been on this ship since we left Okew. You must not have seen her before now."

He considered this for a half second, then smiled. "You're probably right. That's what I get for guessing."

I held his stare. Underneath his smile, his face was still in that politely backed up expression, which told me he wasn't being fully honest either. My experiments were still giving me nothing but daily anxiety attacks, and the situation with the crew was aging like dry rot. It might be time for me to get an outside perspective.

"Amaranth...I'm going to tell you something, but I need you to keep it between us. Okay?"

He looked shocked. "Sure, Reg."

"I met Exia in the cave. She saved my life, and I'm helping her get back home as repayment."

For a minute, his only response was a slight tilt of the head, then he said, "I knew it. I mean, not all that about her saving you, but I definitely knew she wasn't on *this* ship two weeks ago."

"Have you told anybody else about her?"

"Did I tell the group of people who are already threatening to cut each other over soap that there's an extra person on the ship?" He laughed. "This might be my first time stranded in space, but my survival skills are still good."

"Exia won't hurt anybody. She isn't violent."

What did I know? She could be plotting each of our deaths under my bedroom every day, but my gut told me she was here to help. A memory surfaced, unwarranted, of the fish in the tunnels scattering to get out of her way. Not the normal reaction to a nonviolent goddess.

"That's good to know, but there are fifty-eight other people on this ship, and I, for one, don't want them to start thinking how much easier things would be if there were one less person here. They already fixed a drawing to get me out of the room."

"I thought you said you won."

"I did." He sidestepped me and went over to the round daybeds that sat around the river. "I got a nice, comfy spot with a view of the water. This is much better than my cubby bed in research."

"Don't get comfortable."

He stretched out on the chair anyway and folded his arms under his head. "You should take a walk around the ship today to get a read on things for yourself. It'll do you some good to get out of this dark room.

Trust me, after a walk and- nothing personal- a long shower, you'll feel like a new man."

"I'm starting to see why they voted you out."

I TOOK Amaranth's advice and washed my ass before walking the corridor that ran around the ship. The blue lights that framed the wall projections clashed with the bright white lights in the ceiling, and Exia's complaint about them irritating her eyes came back to me. These were probably contributing to my headaches, too, but the commander didn't want to critique my creation, so he gave me that excuse about ship pressure.

I entered the ship crew wing and walked past the commander's sleeping quarters. The control room was right next door. Through the open doors, I spotted the dark control panels and a wide projection screen that showed the desolate land outside. It looked like no one had been in this room in days. A half empty bowl of Ofrran soup from three nights ago sat perched above the call button, and one of the chairs was being used to hang wet clothes on.

A woman's voice traveled out into the corridor from three doors down. She was telling someone off, but I couldn't hear the other person's response. I moved closer to the entryway, not bothering to be sneaky about it. The ship's glossy floors announced you long before you entered a room.

"He can do it himself! They all can," the female voice said.

"It's not their job. It's yours." I was surprised to hear Elmo. His voice was the direct opposite of the woman's. He was in de-escalation mode. "We've been through this, Halle. The rules haven't changed just because our return home has been delayed. You're still expected to handle the meals. That's your duty."

"Nobody else is handling their duties! The ship crew does nothing all day but troubleshoot the same scanners, and the researchers act like we're their servants. Have you *been* in the kitchen? No, none of you have because if you had, you'd know that even without our equipment on, it is unbearable in there. It's so hot that we've been rotating out in shifts of three every fifteen minutes, so no one passes out."

"I didn't know it was that hot in there. I'll look for somewhere–" He paused when I walked in. "Sir?"

I never did answer the question about what they should call me now. I remember giving some rambling answer about not knowing if the lapse in my power was temporary and doing my best not to guarantee anything. I guess they settled on sir.

"Can I talk to you for a minute?" I asked Elmo.

Halle rolled her eyes and stormed off before he could answer. The cobalt blue of her kitchen crew shirt flapped aggressively as she turned the corner into the corridor like it was flipping us off for her. I turned back to Elmo, who looked like I felt before my shower.

"The royal staff was brought on for me. They shouldn't have to keep working if I'm not the king anymore."

"Their work serves another purpose now. They ensure everyone gets an appropriate amount of food each day, so we don't have to worry about enforcing a food ration. If we start letting everyone make their own meals–"

"Right, I get it. I didn't think about that."

Elmo clasped his hands in front of his waist and examined me. He looked down at my clean clothes and freshly trimmed facial hair. After three long seconds of his silent inspection, I reached up to check to see if I had missed a spot shaving. "What?"

"That's all?" He asked.

"What's all?"

"You don't have a suggestion for the kitchen problem?"

"No. What were you going to tell Halle before I came in?"

"Nothing, but I was thinking about changing the schedule to one hot meal a day and have them prepare it during the cooler hours."

"That sounds good." I shrugged. Another weighted silence fell between us. "Is there something you want to say to me, Elmo?"

"I'm sorry, I'm just used to you having a rebuttal."

"What are you talking about? I always follow your plans."

"No. You pretend to listen to my suggestions, and then you do what you want to do, which is usually the exact opposite."

"That's not true. I've followed The Council's lead on everything since day one." Where was this coming from? Elmo was assigned to train me. He had been with me from the beginning. He was usually standing next to me whenever I gave in to one of The Council's 'suggestions'.

He continued to shake his head. "You let us take the lead on things you don't want to deal with: policies, kingdom relations, threats, and energy distribution."

"Because that's what you all *do*." They never failed to tell me how important The Council was to Okew's kingdoms.

"No, sir, it isn't. We find the new king or queen and get him or her acclimated to their new position, but the fate of the kingdom is ultimately up to the person Kani chooses to lead us."

"Then I don't see the problem. You say you want me to step up, but you have a problem when I go with my gut. I don't know what you all want for me. I've been nothing but accommodating to everyone on this ship. I could tell you every health issue they've had and name their relatives in order of importance to them, but as soon as things get messy, when I can't wave my hand and make a rainbow appear for them, all that goes out the window."

Elmo, at least, had the decency to look a little ashamed. I'd been torturing myself, trying to figure out a way to get us off this planet, only to be told that I was not doing enough. He cleared his throat, and I expected an apology was going the next thing out of his mouth. It wasn't.

"Being king isn't about being liked, sir. You could befriend every person in Dewar, and at the end of your life, they'd still say you failed them. And if all you did was ask about their family and how they were doing, then ultimately, they'd be right. What people want from their leaders- from you- is stability. They want to know that if they come to you with legitimate issues, you won't blow smoke in their face or downplay their concerns. They want to know that if they follow you, you won't drag them through the flames and back."

7

Five.

That's the number of names that were drawn. Amaranth from research, Halle and her equally rude prep cook, and two ship crew people who have decided to screw their way through the next two weeks. The guy, Kidran from maintenance, actually asked me if he could sleep in my bed since I'd started spending my nights roaming the corridors. I told him I'd burn the whole thing if I even suspected he'd been in it.

I was done being nice.

It didn't win me any support from the crew, and, like Elmo said, they didn't want nice. They wanted to go home.

I was passing by the greenhouse where we stored the plant samples on my nightly walk, and a familiar pink glow caught my attention. I wandered in and followed the light to where Exia was sitting on the floor, in between the one fume hood we had in here and the two large soil tubs. It was mostly dark, with the only light coming from her and the emergency one in the hood.

She sat with her legs crisscrossed on a blue heating blanket. It was hot enough to melt eyebrow hair on this ship. What was the blanket for?

"Have you been sleeping in here?" I asked.

Exia's gaze started at my bare feet and dragged up my gray pajama pants and t-shirt. By the time she reached my eyes, hers were heavy. It was moments like this and the one in the river that made me question what I originally thought about Exia's feelings towards me and about how close to human the death gods were. She looked like any other woman if you overlooked the insane beauty. Her body was like a human female's, but did she think like them? What did she dream about when she slept? Did she sleep? I'd heard before that dreams were a gateway to a person's desires—a way of experiencing what you couldn't or didn't yet have in real life.

What did Exia desire?

"No, but I can't do this in your room anymore," she responded.

"It's gotten too crowded in there for me, too. What are you doing?"

The glow that radiated around her like a pink flame stuttered before regaining its muted warmth.

"Getting to know this new body of mine."

"Oh. Can I watch?"

Her bottom lip went between her teeth while she considered, and I instinctively licked my own. She looked me over again, this time slower and not hiding her appreciation of my body. When she made it back up to my face again, she waved her hand towards the empty spot in front of her. I quickly scuttled down to the floor, sitting on the heels of my feet with my hands clasped between my spread knees.

She didn't move, but she took a deep breath in, and the pink glow flexed, expanding upward. It was interesting how connected she seemed to be to her power. I always used to have to focus to summon The Gift, and when I did, I held it in my hands like a pool of water. It never radiated from me like hers did. It always felt like something I was wielding, not something that was a part of me.

"So, this isn't what you naturally look like?" I gestured to her shoulders and face.

"No. This body is like a mask. I wear it to fit in in the mortal realm, but it has trouble containing my power sometimes."

"What happens when it can't contain it?"

"It breaks down. I don't let it get to that point."

The soft edges of light danced at my knees, stopping just shy of touching me.

"Can you show me what you do?"

She didn't answer me, but she uncrossed her legs and stood. Taking a couple of steps forward, she kneeled down between my legs, bathing me in her dark, feminine scent and pink glow. Her hair was up in a ponytail, and only the shorter parts in the front were free, framing her face. I wanted all of it down. I wanted to see and feel all of her, with nothing- not even a ponytail holder- getting in my way.

She raised her hand to my face and ghosted it along my cheek, jaw, and chin. Her fingers briefly brushed my skin, and for the first time in days, I welcomed the heat.

It's hard to describe the sensation that overtook me then. It was like in the cave when Exia showed me my death, but this time, I wasn't standing to the side watching myself like an apparition. This time, I was teleported to the meadow that surrounded the southern wing of the palace in Dewar. We were currently in the hot season back home, but the white bark on the tree trunks told me she had taken us to a time during the colder months. The trees and wildflowers swayed with a light breeze that I didn't feel, and everything had a misty glimmer to it.

Exia stood across the way from me, cloaked in a sheer dove-gray fabric. It also billowed in the wind, occasionally clinging to a form underneath. I say form because it wasn't a human body, not really. She had four arms, and through the fabric, I could see her face lacked normal features like a nose and mouth. Instead, there were black feathers. They fanned out, covering all of her face except for two almond-shaped sections where her eyes stared out at me.

This should have been terrifying. I literally should've been falling to my knees and begging her to take me back to my crowded, hot room on the ship, but all I could do was look at her and marvel.

She was the most beautiful thing I had ever seen.

There was a glory to her, a magnificence that didn't exist in us regular mortals. It made you *want* to get down on your knees and worship her. I never would have thought this was who I had been casually talking to all this time. I'd put her out of my room and forced her to stay in a green-house. What the hell was wrong with me?

"Exia, I'm—"

I was interrupted by laughter, a child's laughter. It came from deeper in the meadow, past the purple kerjuva tree leaves, and echoed hollowly in the wind. Before I could ask if she had heard it too, everything around me started to rumble. There was nothing for me to hold on to to brace myself, and it didn't matter anyway because the next thing I knew, the world around us broke. Like a glass that had been thrown to the ground, the meadow fractured into individual pieces that flew apart in slow motion.

Out of the darkness between the broken shards stepped a gigantic shadow man. He - it- was the biggest thing I had ever seen, and my blood instantly turned to cement in my veins. He reached a humongous hand down towards me. It had eight spindly fingers that jerked wildly like ropes caught in a cyclone.

I stumbled back, narrowly avoiding his touch, and fell into an abyss. As I fell, my body twisted in odd ways, sideways and sometimes in reverse. Pieces of the forest drifted past me, each containing some kind of illusion. One was a man carrying books up a flight of stairs that tilted vertically. The other was a large eye that looked like the marble eye of a teddy bear at first, but got more lively and reptilian the longer I looked at it. I continued to fall, and the scenes got more and more bizarre. Through it all, I could feel the shadow man searching for me. I'd lost him when I fell, and now his anger was so palpable I could feel it inside me, like he was in my head somehow.

On a chance, I twisted my body, aiming for one of the scenes. I crashed into a shard that was only slightly bigger than my body and passed into it.

My luck must have been holding up because the world I fell into was a normal one. There were people there, and they gathered around me as soon as I tumbled sideways out of the shard onto a boulder that was twice my height and wide enough to provide shade, which I'm assuming was what the people had been using it for before I showed up.

They all started speaking at once, frantic words that sounded like gibberish to my throbbing ears. The girl closest to me, a young girl, no more than fourteen, pointed at my face and said, "Kaus e lim. Oreja! Orejafefie!"

It kind of sounded like she was saying o-ree, like the Orej Zans that are given to The Gifted by the people of Okew after they die. They were titles that represent that king or queen's legacy as a ruler. Some in the past had been 'Zamin, Morale', 'Kem of the Mighty Harvest', and 'Tasha, The Flight'. Mine would probably be Ormiez, The Reject. I just hoped they waited until after I was dead to announce it.

The people stood back, glaring at me like I was a brown spot on their freshly cleaned t-shirt. Some started backing away from me, shaking their heads. One man turned to the woman next to him and started speaking in quick, angry words. Like with the girl, I was able to pick out one or two that sounded vaguely familiar. Were they speaking Enid? I wasn't fully sure, but there was one way to find out.

I pressed my scraped palms to the boulder and pushed myself up. The crispy yellow grass crunched beneath my feet when I jumped down, reminding me I didn't have shoes on. The people around me may as well have been barefoot, too. The sandals they had made out of wood planks and torn fabric couldn't have been comfortable. Neither could all the mud that was caked on their body from the neck down. It didn't seem to serve a modesty purpose because they had on clothes, gold uniforms with mesh stripes across the front and back. The gold fabric was metallic and gleamed in the late afternoon sun. It looked futuristic if you ignored the craft shoes.

I brushed the dirt off my shirt and pants and looked around for the puzzled face in the crowd. Puzzled was way better than outraged. I could work with puzzled.

I spotted him to my left, standing with his arm stretched out protectively in front of a young boy. He was about my age, but you wouldn't guess it with the wild man beard he was sporting. I took one step back, making sure he knew he was the one in control of this situation.

"My name is Ormiez. I'm...uh...a traveler." *Best to go with that.* "Can you understand what I'm saying?"

I spoke in my most clear Enid, but the man still frowned like I had just said 'can you show me the rice good friendly'. I was about to try again when my body was suddenly jerked backward. The world blurred around me for a second before I found myself back on the ship, with Exia's hand clenched tight around my wrist.

"Why'd you pull me out? I was about to ask them to come save us."

She loosened her grip and sat back. Her pink glow was gone, and for a quick second, when I first opened my eyes, she almost seemed scared.

"They can't save you. They aren't even in the same time as you," she said.

I frowned. "What? I don't...I don't understand."

"The dimension you crossed into was from another life. Those people don't exist anymore. Guardians are not only responsible for the dead. We maintain the balance between life and death in all realms. That means we can't have them interacting with one another. You asked me to show you how I temper my power so it doesn't overtake my human body. I do that by going through the realms and helping souls find rest."

"*You're telling me those people were dead?* I was talking to a bunch of *dead people?*"

"They were alive in that time, but rest is not just death," she said, like that made all the sense.

I dropped my head into my hand, so she wouldn't see how close to freaking out I was. "So, who was the shadow man?"

"Who?"

I took a calming breath and raised my head. "The big ass, angry shadow with the snake fingers? He scared the shit out of me."

Exia looked away for a moment. Her lips parted slightly, and she made a soft gasping noise that made my blood pressure spike.

"I need to do something," she said, jumping to her feet and heading in the direction of the exit to the corridor.

I scrambled up to follow her. "Do what? Where are you going?"

She paused at the door and turned towards me. "Nowhere. I need you to leave. I can't have any distractions right now."

That stopped me in my tracks. "I'm a distraction?"

"Yes."

She looked at me like I was asking something I should have known the answer to already. Should I have known? I'd been so thrown by the effect she had on me, I didn't consider that I might have one on her. While I was thinking back on our interactions so far and grinning from ear to ear, Exia grabbed my hand and pulled me through the open doorway.

"Wait. Can I come back la—," I started to ask, but she pressed her hand to the scanner, and a solid wall formed between us.

8

———

Sijomal Hamp's frog face filled the screen, blocking my view of the small circle of pillows I'd set beneath the stairs in my room before I found out Exia wasn't doing her daily ritual in here anymore.

"Good evening, Elmo. Sir." He must have heard about my new official title. "I've got good news. The rescue ships set out this morning. Sir, yours should be there in five weeks' time. The ship for the rest of the crew should be there shortly after."

"Five weeks?" Elmo's hand crept to the back of his head. "But, Sijomal, it took us three to get here. Can't they expedite things, considering we are surviving on limited supplies?"

Exactly. And why the hell were they just now leaving? It'd been eight days since we told them we were stuck. Then there was the other problem with his 'good news.' "I can't leave everybody here while they wait on the next ship. Why can't they get here at the same time? If anything, I'll stay and wait for the next ship."

"The first ship is a healing crew. We haven't been able to locate the new king or queen of Dewar, so we believe The Gift is still with you. Maybe you have picked up some sickness on that planet, and it is affecting your powers. Elmo tells me you refuse to be looked at by the bolkin."

"I'm not sick, and I'm not going to let that thing feed on me. Especially since it hasn't eaten in weeks."

Hamp chuckled. "It can't harm you. All they do is heal."

"Yeah, well, like I said, I'm not sick."

His oval nostrils flared, giving us a disgusting view from his communicator's low angle. He looked at Elmo and they had a brief, silent conversation. From my conversation with Elmo in the corridor, I could guess what Sijomal Hamp was saying on his end.

"We'll wait for both ships to get here before we leave," I said, disrupting their silent argument. "While we're waiting, the healing medics can check everyone out and see if anyone needs care. There's bound to be some severe cases of dehydration to come up while we sit and wait for five weeks."

Sijomal Hamp looked like he was ready to refuse my suggestion, so I switched strategies.

"You said it's possible The Gift is still with me? That means technically, I'm still king of Dewar."

He looked at Elmo again. This time Hamp's disappointment was aimed at him, and from Elmo's rigid posture and the single coily strand of hair he was trying to hide in his fist, I could tell disappointing his senior would not be overlooked.

"I agree with—," Elmo started to say when the ship moved. Not just the floor, the entire ship moved like it was being picked up. Elmo stopped talking to focus on getting his balance. If I wasn't doing the same thing, I would have told him to keep going because I was almost sure he was about to say he agreed with me. "What's happening?"

Surprisingly, that question was directed at me.

"I don't know," I said.

The ship's launch system hadn't been active in days, but even if it was, this wasn't a bottle rocket that spewed water to get off the ground. The ship shouldn't have been shaking at all.

Another rumble shook the room, this time so hard enough that Elmo and I grabbed each other. He gripped the back of my shirt like he was trying to choke me with it, and I hooked my arm around his front and grabbed his wrist. Sijomal Hamp was yelling on the screen for one of us to tell him what was happening. *Did he not just hear Elmo ask me that and me tell him I didn't fucking know?*

Without warning, the floor dropped out from beneath us. Elmo lost his grip on me as he fell to the ground and went sliding towards my stairs. It was like a scene out of a nightmare. He screamed as he slid down, scrambling for something to hold on to to stop his fall. He found it when his foot caught on the base of the stairs, and his whole body flipped upside down. He crashed into the heavy pots holding my dead plants and slammed head-first into the wall.

"Elmo!" I dropped to my butt and slid down to him. "Elmo? Elmo, can you hear me?"

He was out cold. The ship groaned as it tilted again, this time dipping forward and to the right. Whatever was happening, I needed to get Elmo some place safe. I hoisted him up by his torso. It was awkward because he was a gangly man and taller than me. My legs wobbled, but I managed to get his dead weight onto my shoulder and take one shaky step toward the door.

Something crashed outside in the corridor. It sounded loud, like one of the eating area tables hitting a wall. They were mounted to the floor, but with how hard the ship was rocking, it could have come off. I finally said fuck it and sprinted towards the door. Adrenaline pushed me up the incline and carried me down the corridor. Pure luck kept Elmo from slipping out of my arms. My heart felt like a tambourine, shaking to a frantic beat.

What the hell is happening? Where is everyone?

The corridor was deserted, and I didn't hear anyone in the common area. The temperature chamber from the research wing was turned on its side in the hallway. Its glass door had shattered when it fell, and a large pool of blood ran from the chamber to the end of the corridor. I hiked

Elmo up on my shoulder and kept going. The blood was slippery under my feet, making it even harder to move forward. It tapered off as I got closer to the end, but I left a trail of bloody footprints leading into the other wing.

I shot past the ship's control room, then backtracked when I noticed the commander and his crew were crowded inside. Squeezing in between the bodies, I made my way to the commander. He had his back to me, staring at the screens that were now all on. Each of them showed a different angle of what was happening outside. Of the large sinkhole collapsing beneath the ship.

"Take your stations! Ready in ten!" the commander yelled, throwing his hands wildly at five men who were still frozen in shock.

He was going to try to take off. Even if the control system was working, it would take minutes to get off the ground, and the launch may cause the hole to fall out faster.

"We don't have time for that," I yelled, stopping his stream of commands. "We need to get everyone off the ship."

The commander looked back and forth between me and the controls, hesitating.

"*Commander, now!*"

The crew rushed out into the corridor, solving his dilemma for him. They split into two groups, each heading in different directions, guided by two leaders.

"Take him." I handed Elmo to the commander. "I'll make sure everyone gets out."

He nodded to let me know he was finally on board with my plan, so I turned and ran back out.

I hit the corridor at top speed. People crashed into me as they ran in the opposite direction, towards the exit. The ship was rocking with every dip it took into the ground, sending people stumbling into walls and through open doorways. Someone fell to my left, a man. He hit the floor with a loud oomph and immediately rolled onto his side and covered his face with his arms. I didn't understand what he was doing until I realized no one was stopping. The flood of bodies continued to push forward, blocking each of his attempts to get up. All eyes were on the woman up ahead who was directing people towards the exit, so they didn't notice that one of their own had fallen. He yelled for help over the cacophony of voices, reaching a hand out for someone to pull him up, but no one did. *I shouldn't stop for him either,* I thought. Going back for him could mean me not getting to the rest of the crew in time to warn them.

But if I didn't do something, they were going to trample him to death.

I pressed my back against the corridor wall and pushed off. At that same moment, the ship tilted again, and everyone went crashing into the other wall. I almost tripped over the guy but managed to step over him at the last second. Once I had him up, I realized it was Fred from the research team.

He stared at me in shock, visibly trembling. Instead of asking if he was okay, I spun him around by his shoulders and shoved him towards the exit.

I needed to find Exia. She was still on the ship. I don't know how I knew, but I just did. I felt it, and every minute I didn't have eyes on her was one where I couldn't breathe.

"Exia!"

A flash of beige and brown caught my eye as she stepped into the common area from the hallway that led to the communal showers.

"Exia." My chest loosened as I ran to her.

"I didn't do this," she said calmly.

What's messed up is I didn't even have time to feel like shit over that comment, but I made a mental note to make it up to her later on if we got out of this alive.

"I know, but I need your help. Can you keep us stable until I get everyone off the ship?"

Her eyes got big, and she took a big step back. *What's this?* I had never seen Exia unsure about anything before. She was always so cool under pressure that I think I had convinced myself that was her default. It occurred to me, then, that what I was asking her to do had to be a major conflict. There was probably a rule that forbade her from helping us.

That was the only explanation I could think of for why she was hesitating.

"You can't do it," I asked.

"I can, but," she paused and weighed her words, "The W'aminsa is about sacrifice. I told you that before. Your powers didn't mean much to you, but obviously, your crew does. Maybe this is your test, and not all of them are meant to survive it."

So her hesitation was about the W'aminsa, but not in the way I had thought.

"No," I shook my head. "Absolutely *fucking* not. What kind of game is this? I'm not about to let my people fall into a hole and die to appease some bloodthirsty gods."

The floor took a hard dip, and I stumbled into a table, banging my hip on the round edge. Exia stood like a statue in the middle of the chaos. The rocking ship didn't seem to faze her at all. But her face as she stared down at me? The utter sadness blanketing her beautiful features? It nearly broke me. She was trapped here, too. If I let a few people die, she could go back to her life as a goddess, and I would have my powers back. This should've been an easy decision. She'd given me my life back. It was only right that I do the same for her.

But I was a virus, and not even death gods were immune.

"Please, Exia." I dropped to my knees before her. If I had to beg, I would beg. "Don't make me choose. I'll do anything else. I'll stay behind when they go back to Okew, and I promise I'll spend every minute of every day finding a way to get you back to your old life. I just can't do this. Not this way. I'm... I'm sorry."

I bowed my head, unable to face the disappointment I knew would be there from now on when she looked at me. No wonder she never gave me a chance. Maybe deep down, she knew that I'd only fail her.

For what felt like an hour, she didn't say anything to me. I was about to tell her to get off the ship and go find whoever else I could when the floor stopped shaking. As quickly as the sinkhole opened and jump started this whole disaster, Exia had brought it all to a standstill.

"Thank you." I jumped up and pulled her into my arms. "Thank you."

That was all the relief I allowed myself to feel before letting go of Exia and sprinting out the door toward the staff sleeping quarters. I barreled through the rows of cubby beds, scanning the top row on my way in and the bottom on my way out.

"Is anyone in here? We need to get off the ship right now! It's safe to come out, but you need to come now!"

The rooms were clear, but when I passed the kitchen, I heard voices.

"You all need to get out right now," I said to the four men grabbing armfuls of food from the supply closet and tossing them into compression boxes. Thankfully, they had filled the boxes to the max and were about to leave anyway.

I found one person in the showers- he claimed he didn't feel the ship rocking- and another three huddled up together in a small media room. They'd been too afraid to make a run for it.

I finished checking the rest of the ship and looked down the corridor towards the exit to make sure the seven people I'd found were on their way out before going back for Exia. She was still standing in the common room.

"Let's go." I held my hand out.

The instant she slid her hand in mine, the floor collapsed, and time stopped as we went flying through the ship at zero gravity. My back slammed against the wall of the corridor, and Exia collided with my front a second later, knocking the wind out of me. I wrapped one arm around her waist and used my other to protect her head from the objects flying out of the rooms.

"I'm going to roll us towards the exit," I yelled over her head.

Walking out wasn't an option anymore. I don't know what happened, but Exia no longer had control over the sinkhole. We had maybe seconds to get out before we were swallowed alive. I kicked off the wall, holding one hand out to keep from crushing her with my weight.

We rolled nine times before tumbling into the little anteroom where the exit was. My left shoulder was throbbing, and I was pretty sure one of my knees had popped out of place during the roll. I used a nearby wall to push myself back up, thanking Kani that I was able to stay on my feet.

Above our heads, the exit door was clear, and all I could see was reddish-gray soil. We had fallen so deep into the ground that the sky had disappeared.

I grabbed Exia by the waist anyway and lifted her above my head. When she was out the door, I grabbed the frame and hoisted myself up, too.

"Someone else is coming out!" a woman cried from the top of the hole. She and forty other people stared down at us from way too far up.

They can't reach us.

The realization was like a shot to the heart, and it was clear from all the solemn expressions above that they were thinking the same thing.

"I got an idea." I crouched down in front of Exia. "Get on my shoulders. If they can reach you, they'll pull you out."

She looked at me in shock, then slowly shook her head.

"There's no point in both of us dying." I grabbed her hand and tried to get her to see reason. "I made my choices. I don't know if they were the right choices, but here we are. And now I'm choosing you. Let me save you for once."

She stopped shaking her head and looked down at her hand in mine. Something flashed across her face, and she climbed on my shoulders without a word. As soon as she was on, I stood up. *They'll be able to reach her now.* I moved to the side, using the ship's slanted position to gain more height, and yelled up at the people still watching us from the top of the hole. "Somebody grab her hands!"

Exia's calves slipped under my armpits, and she brought her feet together behind my back. She did it so fast that I had to wonder if she had practiced this hold before.

"Hold on to me," she said, patting her thighs.

My first instinct was to tell her no. They couldn't lift us both. But she gave me that same determined look she had while looking at our joined hands a moment ago. And, man, she was gorgeous in her bossy goddess mode. I would have done anything she asked me to, so I wrapped my forearms around her calves, but mentally I told myself that if she couldn't carry my weight or they couldn't pull us both up, I would let go.

Exia grunted, and I felt myself being lifted up. Tug after excruciating tug, she let out harsh breaths through her nose. I could feel her muscles straining everywhere we were connected. This was physical torture for her and psychological for me.

Please hurry.

Something popped. In the enclosed space, it sounded louder than the temperature chamber hitting the corridor wall. Exia looked towards the sky and let out a guttural scream. Her legs started to shake, and I closed my eyes, preparing myself to let go.

The voices of the crew grew closer, and soon a stale breeze wafted over my face. I opened my eyes and looked up just as three pairs of hands reached into the hole, grabbing Exia's shirt while the two people holding her arms pulled her the rest of the way up.

"Be careful. I think we might have pulled her arm out of the socket," I heard one of them say. Then I was being dragged up by my waistband.

We hit the ground, and I couldn't think. I crawled on instinct, getting as far away from the sinkhole as my quivering arms and legs would take me before collapsing onto my stomach.

"*Exia!*" I screamed into the dirt.

"I'm here," her voice came from somewhere on my right, weaker than I had ever heard it.

"Where?" I reached out, blindly grasping for her. My fingers brushed against fabric, and I quickly closed my fist around it.

She was there.

She had made it.

We had made it.

I only had enough strength left to turn my head to look at her. She was on her back, staring up at the sky, and her stomach was rising and falling hard against my fist, which had a tight grip on her shirt. Her shoulder didn't look out of place, but she was being very still. I let go, and my hand dropped to her side to see if she'd respond. She knew what I needed, even if I wasn't capable of asking for it right then. Her fingers slid beneath mine, barely close enough to be considered touching, but it was enough.

A short distance behind Exia, the crew stood huddled together, watching the last of our ship and everything on it disappear into the hole.

9

———

I wouldn't say I was happy the bolkin was here, but we had twelve injured people, one dislocated finger, and numerous 'something is wrong. My vision keeps going in and out' complaints. Fred was all bruised up from his near trampling, and Elmo was still unconscious.

The mass vision loss was probably hysteria. One or two of them seemed legit, but hopefully, they would recover once the panic wore off- if it wore off. We were still stranded, but now we were stranded without shelter. Once that sunk in, shit was bound to go from bad to worse. For now, all I could do was tell them to breathe and try to relax.

As for the other injuries, the bolkin was all we had. Our healing supplies were buried with the remains of our ship. From my position beneath one of the metal tripod things that showed up when Exia reversed time to revive me, I watched the bolkin's white mist body pass over the group of injured people who had been separated from everyone else.

It came to a stop over Elmo's sagging head.

A man and a woman stood on either side of him with his arms slung over their shoulders. As the mist expanded and lowered, covering them from the waist up, red spread across it. Bright red at first, but then it deepened to the color of blood. Where Elmo's head was shrouded, there was a spot of black.

I waited for the bolkin to rise and move on to the next person, but one minute passed and then another. The mist didn't move.

Bolkin healing wasn't something that could be easily predicted. How quickly they healed depended on a lot of things: how serious the injury was, the health and age of the bolkin, how hungry it was. Ours should've been starving, but I had no idea what shape it was in health-wise. So maybe it was taking so long because the bolkin was no good.

Another minute passed, and the mist finally lifted and moved away from Elmo. His skin was pale, like the bolkin had fed on his blood instead of his injury, and his head lolled on his shoulders. The woman on his right said something to the man that I couldn't hear. He pressed two fingers to Elmo's neck and shook his head.

I pushed off the metal pole I was leaning against and strode over to the injured group at a controlled but fast pace. I didn't want to alert everyone else, but watching the woman gaze worriedly over Elmo's head had caused a chill to run down my spine.

I'd fucked up. I should have told the commander to put the bolkin on him as soon as they made it off the ship. I didn't even check to see if he was still breathing after he'd hit his head. Now he'd been unconscious- probably without oxygen- for who knew how long.

I spotted Exia out of the corner of my eye, far away from the group. She had her eyes closed, and her head was tilted toward the sky. It looked like she was praying, though I don't know who a goddess would pray to.

I got to Elmo and checked his pulse and found nothing. No, wait. It was there, but very faint.

I'll take it.

"Keep an eye on him, and after the bolkin finishes this round, have it come back and stay on Elmo until he wakes up."

The guy nodded. "Yes, sir."

I squeezed Elmo's hand- which was, thankfully, still warm- before crossing the rocky terrain to where Exia was. She didn't acknowledge me when I walked up, but her eyes opened. They were glued to the outline of the portal in the sky. Honestly, I was amazed it was still there. Without my power to sustain it, I thought it would wear down over time like the ship. She lifted her hand slowly toward it, and her fingers curled in. The portal immediately started to shrink. I turned to see if anyone was watching, and sure enough, everyone was. All eyes were on the portal- which looked like a black circle in the sky without stars or thunderclouds around to define it- as it got smaller and smaller. The commander pushed to the front of the crowd, looking from the portal to Exia to me. If telepathy was a thing, he had just unlocked his ability because I heard 'this is all your fault' from where I was, some forty feet away.

"Exia, what are you doing?" I reached out to grab her hand and get her to stop or just *look* at me, help me understand where her head was. She jerked away from me, or at least I thought it was from me, until the wave of heat hit the side of my face, and I realized the portal was gone.

For the second time that day, the terrified cries of my crew filled the air.

"She's going to kill us!"

"He brought her here! This is his fault!"

"Please. We didn't do anything. Please!"

Exia ignored their screams and put her finger beneath my chin, turning my head to the left. "Look."

There was a collection of rock pillars along the horizon. They went far back, covering the entrances to the tunnels and sloping down into a rocky valley. The one Exia pointed out was taller than the others, and the top of it was rounded like a half-moon. Shadows ghosted along the rock face as the clouds moved freely now, without the portal there to absorb them.

I was about to ask what I was supposed to be looking at when thousands of tiny light beams hit the pillar at the same time. They came from all over, and a few were coming from the direction of the sinkhole. I turned and scanned the field, trying to find the source, when a flicker winked from the top of the tripod I'd been standing beneath earlier. Around it, all the other tripods reflected light toward the pillar, too. At first, I thought they were all the same, but now I realized there were slight differences in their heights and shape. It was so minute that, had I not witnessed this light show, I never would have known otherwise. But they all pointed at the large pillar.

The shadows filled two craggy ovals near the top of the towering rock, giving it black eyes that looked out over the land. More shadows gathered in random places between the lights, carving out long limbs and facial features. It was a crude rendition, but I had seen that stance before and those black, all-consuming eyes. Anyone who had been to Dewar's Hall of The Gifted had. The place where we kept paintings of all the past rulers of our people.

"That's Xeonere, the first king," I stated needlessly. I was pretty sure everyone else had figured out who was embedded in the tall pillar by some complicated light system that I couldn't even begin to figure out.

"Yes, this was where he and his people lived," Exia responded.

"The travelers? This was one of the planets they visited?"

I'd thought that when I first saw Exia, but to have physical confirmation. And not just any group of travelers. This was the group that Xeonere himself traveled with. The Council was going to lose their shit when they heard about this.

"No." Exia shook her head. "This was their original planet."

"What?" All the excitement drained from me and sizzled in a puddle on the overheated ground. This was their original planet, the one they had depleted in a failed attempt to satisfy Xeonere's ego. Like everyone in Okew, I'd heard the stories about how he had forced his people to create monuments to him all over the planet, but I had no idea how advanced these things were. I figured they were hauling bricks and carving out stones with hand tools.

"Creating something like this takes a lot of precision and calculation," Exia said, staring at the monument like it was a mass grave.

"I bet."

"Xeonere didn't have much patience for calculation, so he had his people act as the prisms. They dressed in light-reflecting clothes and moved around in the daylight until they figured out the precise locations for where to build the structures."

Light-reflecting clothes. An image surfaced in my mind of people in gold uniforms with mud caked all over their exposed skin.

"The dead people?" I whispered. "The ones I saw the other night?"

"They weren't dead then."

"But they died eventually. After Xeonere and his followers left them behind on a dying planet." No wonder they looked so pissed off when I fell into their world. "Wait, I had my powers when I saw them. A girl pointed at my eyes and said `Orej'."

"Yes. You've had power in every one of your lives."

"Every one of my lives? What are you talking about?"

"You have many realms and timelines in your sol dimension, and in each, you've had power of some kind. I thought it was strange at first, as most mortals only have one or two lives, but then you told me about the shadow man, and it all clicked."

I raised my brows when she didn't say anything else.

"Exia," I rubbed at the tension forming between my eyebrows, "I am a fairly smart man, but I obviously don't know as much as you do, not even a fraction. So I need you to be very straightforward with me. What are you saying happened when I was in that place?"

"That place was your sol dimension, and those timelines were all your lives. You are Ormiez in this one, but in another, you were Chaz-achike, and another, you were Xeonere. You seem to have a thing for complicated names."

Exia smiled at her own joke. And if I wasn't busy falling apart, I might have enjoyed that little bit of sunshine. But I was stuck on one thing she'd said.

I was Xeonere.

10

_____

"They don't trust you," Exia said as soon I walked back over to her side of the field.

Everyone was giving her a wide berth, even Amaranth, who claimed to have known what Exia was the minute she boarded the ship. I guess suspecting someone had power was different from seeing it with your own eyes.

"Can you blame them? Everything I've done so far has only brought them lower." And they didn't even know about the stuff I did in my past life as Xeonere. "I'm not the only one they don't trust."

Exia clutched her chest and sputtered. "But I'm Death. Mortals are usually breaking their necks to be around me."

I stopped stressing over the situation with my team to gape at her.

"Man. That was..._dark_." I couldn't help but laugh.

She shrugged, giving me the cutest evil smile in return. What did it say about me that at a time like this and after a joke like that, all I wanted to do was kiss that villain grin? Apparently, it said I had a thing for bad girls and lacked self-control because the next minute, my lips were on hers.

Her hands came up to cradle my face, and she..._melted_ into my arms. Exia was no timid kisser. I never expected her to be. She put her all into everything from the moment she decided you were who she wanted to do it for. I was just lucky she wanted to do this with me.

My arms found their way around her waist on their own and pulled her close, not even leaving room for air between us. I wanted every part of her touching me, from her delicious lips to her perfect toes. She dragged her fingers down my arms and slipped them beneath my shirt to trace the muscles in my lower back, and I came alive. This was at the same time her tongue snuck out to meet mine.

This day- hell, every day since we got here- had been a fucking disaster, but this. Her. I could relive this mission over and over and still be happy, as long as it ended like this.

She pulled back and ghosted her lips over mine.

"Where are you going?" I whispered, opening my eyes to see my goddess up close.

Her lashes were like dark wings resting on her round cheeks. Still as perfect as the first time I saw her, but now I took comfort in it because I'd seen her goddess form, so I knew this wasn't some well-designed mask. She was just this beautiful.

I let her pull away, but I took both her hands in mine. "Thank you for trying to cheer me up."

"Trying?" She pulled back and looked me up and down in a way that was so human I laughed again.

I squatted, getting down on the ground, and Exia followed, kneeling in between my legs like she'd done in the greenhouse. I couldn't resist brushing her bangs out of her face and running my thumb across her cheek. I didn't get to do this last time, and now, as Exia brought her hand up to hold mine against her face, I see I was missing out. "I'll be happy when I get you and everyone else off this planet."

She nodded and said, "Fair. Are you ready?"

I took a deep breath. "Yeah"

In the next blink, I was surrounded by darkness. I couldn't smell the grass in the meadows like I did the first time, and there was a slight metallic taste in my mouth.

"Exia?"

My voice echoed back to me, along with the sound of water droplets trickling against stone. That was my first clue to where I was. A moment later, when my eyes adjusted, I got my confirmation.

I was back in the cavern.

A speck appeared on my chest and then grew, glowing brighter and illuminating more of the cave for my eyes to see. It came from the diving suit and mask I now had on, but up ahead, the cave walls danced with fluorescent waves of magenta. I headed that way.

There was much water in this section of the cave. It only covered the bottoms of the rocks and flowed downward like a stream to some other place. Cave floors were filled with pitfalls, and this one was no different. One wrong step could leave you with a twisted ankle or worse, so I took my time jumping from rock to rock. I got to the small opening at the end of the cave and had to get down on all fours to squeeze through.

I crawled out into another cave that had tunnel openings in the floor, at least thirty of them. They were all identical in size and separated by a small strip of dry land barely big enough for one person to walk across. I took a step forward, then waited to see if everything around me would break apart like it did the last time.

Nothing moved besides the magenta waves reflecting on the crags in the ceiling. They came from the water in the tunnels. I walked out onto one of the dry strips, literally having to put one foot in front of the other like I was on a slack line.

The tunnel entrance to my left was muted, but inside its pink water, there were two people hugging, a man and a woman. The woman looked like she was using every muscle in her body to hold on to the guy. After he managed to gently pry her arms from around his neck, he bent down and kissed her cheek before turning to get on the train behind them. There were no tracks beneath the train. It seemed to be floating in midair.

The silver door opened, revealing another man inside the train. His gaze drifted between the two people he couldn't seem to care less about, not even the woman who was crying her eyes out. He stepped to the side and allowed the younger man to board the train, and the doors immediately closed behind him. Train guy put his hand on the other man's shoulder, and light flashed, momentarily blanketing the oval windows of the train. When it receded, the man was alone on the train. There was no sign of the younger one, and the woman dropped to her knees, sobbing.

I took another step forward and peered into another tunnel. In this one, a group of people dressed in light blue robes bowed before a man who sat with his back to them. He was dragging his fingers across a large tapestry that floated in front of him. One of the people in robes shuffled forward on his knees, keeping his head down the entire time. He paused a significant distance away from the guy who by now I'd figured out was me, and dropped something in a gold dish before backing up. Whatever it was he'd put on the plate, I'd never seen it before, but as soon as it clattered in the dish, the tapestry artist's fingers stopped moving, and bright sunlight filtered into the room.

The next tunnel was an abstract scene. Just bony fingers jabbing at a patch of dry, cracked dirt. They dug out a small hole about the size of a coin and poured some kind of green liquid in. Five insects floated out of the hole, frantically wiggling. My stomach turned as I thought about what the nasty-looking bugs were probably used for.

The tunnel to my right was a war zone. Hundreds of people decked out in black armor ran across an open field. They swung their weapons wildly in the air at nothing. My view of them was far away, like I was watching through someone else's eyes, and he was nowhere near the field. I was about to move on to the next tunnel when a white, scaly, snake-like creature came out of the sky. It opened its mouth and scooped up a line of soldiers before retreating back into the clouds. Some of the fighters attacked, stabbing it and throwing spiked wire around the creature, while others ran to avoid being swallowed up. Through it all, my vantage point didn't move.

Up ahead was another battle scene. This one was between a crew of sailors and an army of gory-looking sea creatures. The sailors were extremely outnumbered, and the monsters were using their tails to tilt the boat. Bodies went flying into the water and were instantly dragged into the ocean. My viewpoint was from below this time. I watched a person fall into the water right in front of me before the tunnel went black.

They went on like this. People dying in battle while I watched through cold, unfeeling eyes. A mother begging to be allowed to go home and care for her sick child. Broken, weary expressions. Starvation. Sadness. Hopelessness. All different scenarios, sometimes with non-human creatures, but they all had one common theme: others suffering because I was their leader.

I decided to stop torturing myself, and just fucking sat down. I wrapped my arms around my knees so I wouldn't accidentally enter one of the worlds and hung my head. Surrounded by all my failures, an eternity of devastation, I finally understood why my powers were taken from me. I hadn't hurt anyone yet, but given time, I would have. I still didn't understand why they sent Exia. Why save someone whose only purpose in life so far had been tormenting others? Why not just let me die? I thought about that shit until my ears were ringing from all the back and forth in my head.

Why didn't they let me die?

There had to be a reason. Exia said I was meant for something more. She also said the W'aminsa was always about sacrifice. I'm sure my sacrifice wasn't my crew. I'd done enough indirect killing to last several lifetimes. So what was it? What did I need to give up to earn the gods' approval? What would others say they wished was different about me?

This would have been a good question for my crew if I'd known before I needed to ask it. They'd probably say they wished *I* was different, that Kani had chosen someone else altogether. And I couldn't be mad at that. Plenty of times over the past four months, I'd wished the same thing. But complaining about being king wasn't going to take my life back to what it used to be.

Still, even though I never said it out loud, I always viewed my crown as a burden, as well as the people I now had to lead. They were obstacles in my way of me doing the things I actually wanted to do, always coming to me with some new complaint or need. It was never-ending. And I was supposed to do this for the rest of my life? What happened to taking initiative, to doing what needed to be done for yourself instead of waiting on someone else to do it? *I* gave my all to *my* people. Hell, I nearly got swallowed by a sinkhole trying to get all of them to safety. And in return, I got more distrust, more accusatory stares. They should have been thanking me. No, they should have been thanking the gods for me!

Icy wind swept in the cave with the suddenness of a thunderclap. It hit me hard, knocking me onto my back and tossing my feet in the air. The cave had vanished. Now, all around me, tendrils of black shadows whipped through the air. My arms and legs were stretched tight, being pulled by some unseen force until I was laid out in an X formation.

The shadows rose in a wild flurry, taking the shape of the man who'd stalked my nightmares every night since the first night I'd seen him. His hair was like black flames, twisting angrily on top of a slender head and face, and a dark aura surrounded his body like Exia's pink glow, but also not like her at all. There wasn't anything calming or welcoming about this titan or his power. You'd have to be crazy, blind, and foolish to think that.

My muscles trembled, and my body buckled under the weight of his power. He could have ground me to dust with just a thought, I was sure of it, but instead he set me down at his feet in a kneeling position. My head was forced down further until my forehead dug into my knees. My hands were pulled forward. I tried to fight against the hold he had on me, but it was no use. I had a better chance of breaking out of an airtight metal box.

A sharp pinch on my arms caused me to jerk and cry out. It felt like a piece of my skin had been ripped off. I rolled my eyes up, trying to see the damage for myself, but I couldn't move my damn head. Another pinch came to the arch of my foot. This one was quicker, but more intense. The difference was like someone pricking your finger and then shoving a knife in your foot. Again, as the initial pain retreated, it seemed to take a piece of me with it. He did this four more times, methodically ripping pieces of skin from my body, before I couldn't take anymore.

"Please! I'll do what you want, just stop! I can't...I can't take anymore." I panted into my knees.

My skin felt raw, and my whole body was vibrating. I couldn't even collapse. I was stuck in this position with my hands stretched towards his feet. How long would this go on? More importantly, how much of it would I be alive for?

Three spindly fingers wrapped around the back of my neck and pulled me up to my knees. The shadow man stared down at me from his impossible height.

He took a step forward, and for a moment, I thought he was going to step on me and crush the life out of me like a bug. His foot came down next to my body, not making a sound. He got down on one knee and leaned toward my face.

It was like staring into a black hole.

Every thought and emotion in my body ran for cover. I'd thought this before- many times over the past few days- but this time, I was sure this was the end for me, and with death came clarity. I finally understood what the gods wanted from me.

Acknowledgment.

I had been given so much power, and each time, I acted like it was a shitty birthright. Worse, I'd punished the people I was supposed to be helping because they didn't worship me. I wasn't their god. I wasn't even a lesser god. I just wish I could have figured it out sooner.

11

I wanted my last thoughts to be of Exia, so I closed my eyes and blocked out everything around me, including the shadow man. If I concentrated hard enough, I could almost feel her presence. I could imagine it was her hand wiping the tears from my face. She would stay with me and guide me through whatever came next if the gods allowed her to. I really didn't want to go through this alone. I wasn't sure if I'd make it without Exia.

"Look at me, Ormiez."

Her voice was warmth to my exposed and shivering soul. It gave me the strength I needed to keep fighting against the shadow man's hold. He wouldn't stop me from getting to her. No one would.

"I can't see. Everything's dark."

"Then open your eyes," she laughed.

Exia's laugh...it was the sexiest thing I'd ever heard. Even while trapped in an existential paradox, it made my body stand at attention.

Something pressed into my left eyelid and forced it open. Exia smiled at me, a beaming smile that could have formed its own solar system. She let go of my eyelid and sat back on her heels. The planet's stale air filled my nose, and realized I wasn't in the cave anymore. There was also no sign of the shadow man when I looked around. The world looked different, however, more vivid and defined. Night had fallen while I was in my trance, being punished, and my crew was nowhere in sight.

"Where is everyone?"

"They found an empty cave beneath the statue. It was just big enough for a handful of people, so they're letting the injured recover there while everyone else scouts for permanent shelter, but that won't be necessary anymore."

"Why not?"

She brought her hand back to my face and used her thumb to trace my under eye. "Welcome back, King."

It took me longer than normal to catch on to what she was saying. I raised my hand slowly and, for the first time in days, tried to summon The Gift.

This felt different, too. For one, it came easier now than it had before. I kept it simple, creating a mirror smaller than my palm. It was enough for me to see one glowing eye looking back at me. My eyes with The Gift were usually an amber color. Now they were closer to gold.

I dropped the mirror and watched it hit the ground and shatter into three pieces.

That was real.

I had created something real, using only my power, and it made me sick inside.

"I don't get it."

"Get what?" Exia asked, having heard me whisper my thought out loud.

"Why didn't he kill me? Why spare me again, *and* give my powers back? I'm just going to mess it up again. I mean, how many people is he willing to let die because of me?"

The more I thought about it, the more upset I got. I knew it was irrational. I should've been happy to get another chance at life. But after seeing all my past lives and everything I had done to my own people, I couldn't help but feel like this was a disaster waiting to happen.

Exia scooted forward and pressed her forehead to mine. I exhaled, letting her distract me from my worries, at least for a little while. My eyes drifted closed, and soon Exia's quiet voice filled the night. In my head, I imagined that instead of sitting on the ground outside, we were in bed, and she was telling me about her day.

"I didn't tell you this before, but I used to come sit under your stairs every day to get away from the other mortals. I've never spent this much time in the presence of people who weren't transitioning. They're very confusing. Like one time, I had overheard these two women talking. One was complaining about the weight she had put on since getting stranded here. The other woman said she understood because she had been stress eating too. But then the guy who always reads in the common area turned to both of them and said, 'The workout room is still functional.' They both got upset with him and started shouting. I'm not going to say I don't get why what he said was offensive, but I'd heard the woman inviting her friend to work out with her before, and she always refuses."

Exia made a face like this was the most baffling thing ever. I guess to her- a divine being who's never had to save face- it was.

"That's what makes us human. We're messy and do things ass-backward, but sometimes it's with good intention."

"Hmm." She dragged her fingers along my hand, tracing the vein that went from my wrist to my index finger. "Maybe that's your answer. Kani spared you because you *are* mortal. You know how they think, and you have compassion when they do things the wrong way. Now, you need to offer yourself that same compassion so you can move forward."

It FELT great to wield my power again. I worked through the night, creating any and everything I could think of. This ship was going to be three times better than our old one, and it would get back to Okew in days, not weeks. I was calculating the density needed for the shield that would surround the ship when footsteps approached from behind.

"This is...amazing," Elmo said, eyeing the massive ship in front of us, "but where are the doors?"

I tapped my wristband to close the projection screen and turned toward him. He was standing on his own now, and his doe eyes were wide and alert.

"I'm glad to see you up and about, Elmo." I patted his shoulder, accidentally getting more dirt on his already dingy gray shirt.

"Thank you, Your Highness." He smiled and bowed his head briefly.

"There won't be any doors on this one. I'm sealing it off and putting a shield around it to prevent the ship from warping when we reach maximum speed. You all will get on and off the ship using this." I pulled the marble-sized ball of light from my pocket and handed it to him. "You crush it, and it forms a doorway outside of the ship. Then you just step through to get on."

Elmo's lips thinned as he looked from me to the orb. "This creates portals?"

"Yeah. It's a bit of The Gift in a convenient shell."

"And you are going to give this out? Like it's a present?"

"No, only you and the commander will use them. They also act as fuel for the new ship. I want you to save one to show to The Travel Committee when you get back to Dewar."

"You aren't coming back with us?"

"No. I'm gonna stay here to clean up this planet and tear down these old monuments. Erosion has done some of the work for me, but the metal ones are drawing heat to the surface and preventing new plant growth."

Elmo gazed thoughtfully at one of the dim tripods in the distance. "What are the odds that the first planet we travel to is the one our ancestors and the first king lived on? It's incredible luck."

"I wouldn't call it that, but it does seem like fate led us here."

Led me here.

I obviously couldn't tell Elmo about my intervention with the gods. He'd believe it; *that* I was sure of. But I'd also have to tell him why Kani himself had to step in and backhand some sense into me. I already had a long hill up ahead of me in regaining my crew's trust and finding the descendants of the people I'd doomed in my life as Xeonere. I wasn't trying to create more obstacles for myself.

"Can you let the commander know the ship's ready for its first trial run? I want to run as many tests as we can before we head out."

"Yes, Your Highness." Elmo bowed again, at the waist this time, and turned to head back to the caves.

~

"I just smash it?"

"Yes, you don't have to apply a lot of force. It'll break easily, and the orb will activate from there."

The commander closed his fingers around the orb and squeezed. I was probably the only one who heard it break, and only because I was standing right next to him. Gold sparks materialized a foot in front of us and quickly multiplied. As they rained down, forming an illuminated doorway, the skeptical silence of the crew shifted to wonder.

"Skies above," the commander said, reaching a hand out to test the doorway.

"Ah, Ah. I'll go first," I said. I took one step into the portal and gave the crew a thumbs-up before coming back out.

The commander was next. He sucked in a deep breath, then stepped through the portal. When he came back out in one piece, people hustled forward, ready to get on so we could hurry up and leave. As everyone boarded the ship, Exia came to stand by my side.

"What happens now?" I asked.

"With what?" She tilted her head to look up at me.

"The W'aminsa. I got my powers back, but you're still here. Not that I'm complaining. I just...want to know what you need from me."

"I can leave. There's nothing holding me back from continuing with the Doquime ima Sol, but I've decided to stay in this realm a little longer.

I think I've been away from the living too long and grown out of touch. My jokes don't land like they used to."

I laughed while building up the nerve to ask what I really wanted to know. "So what does that mean for us- me and you?"

She smiled that dark, beautiful villain smile and said, "It means I get to see how the king of Dewar really lives."

EPILOGUE
EXIA'S POV

Life is good.

I spend my days traveling to distant worlds or quaint markets in Dewar's inner kingdom. Then, at the end of the day, my mortal/spiritual husband and I return to our palace, safely nestled in an enchanted forest. We could be a fairytale.

I'd been in Dewar for eight months now, the longest Ormiez and I have ever stayed in one location. He was taking this second chance seriously, doing all he could to make amends for his past mistakes. That meant traveling from planet to planet to find the descendants of the original travelers and offering any help he could.

I was happy to be by his side through it all. It brought me in contact with some interesting mortals and a few gods and goddesses who had also chosen this life among the people. Not long ago, I would have called them crazy or overly sentimental. What god would willingly choose to walk among the mortals? They were- to use Ormiez's word- 'messy' and they sometimes treated common decency like it was a limited resource, only giving it out to those most deserving of it. That's not even mentioning the conflict of knowing how and when they'll die.

Despite all this, I'd grown attached to quite a few of them. For every reason I had for not being in the mortal realm, I'd found a hundred others for staying here. My biggest reason was still yet to come.

I took the north hallway to the private garden, sure that was where Ormiez had disappeared to. He was crouched down, cutting an herb, when I opened our bedroom doors to the garden.

"I knew I'd find you here. I'm guessing the meeting with The Council didn't go well?"

"Same stuff. They want me to push for the descendants to let us keep orb pods on their planets. They think the alliances have been one sided so far, with me finding planets for the travelers who still haven't settled anywhere and them giving nothing in return."

"What did you say to that?"

"What I told them before. The choice is up to the natives of the planet. If they say no, I won't force it. That's not why I'm doing this."

I nodded, even though he wasn't looking at me. He was so focused on taking care of his babies.

"What's that?" I pointed to the plant he'd just pulled out of the ground.

"Gamba Kret, it helps with labor pain."

There were four rows of orange leaves, identical to the one in hand, spanning the garden.

"How much pain do you think I'm going to be in?" I asked, running a hand over my swollen stomach.

"I don't know. Hopefully, none if the GK does its job. Big babies run in my family, and Red here is going to be the biggest and strongest of them all."

He'd taken to calling our unborn child Red because he or she gave me constant heartburn.

Ormiez went over to the outdoor sink to wash the herb, and as always, I took the opportunity to appreciate his body. His sculpted back was covered by the light cream sweater he'd paired with dress pants for his meeting with The Council. He had put on weight since we started traveling, bulking up and training with the guards during his free time at home. I understood his reasoning. Though he always came in peace and only to offer his help, not all of the travelers were welcoming.

He dropped the herb into one of the drying chambers when he was finished rinsing it, then came over and put his face right in front of mine. This was reason number one for me living in the mortal realm. Ormiez loved to kiss me when I was smiling, and he knew the best way to get a smile out of me was one of these human staring contests he insisted I'd be great at. I cracked first, and he came in to collect his prize. I could always feel my husband's sol. It was as familiar to me as my own human body's sol. But when we kissed, the two connected.

He got down on his knees, clearly not bothered by the fact that he was ruining another pair of pants with gardening soil. The seamstress was going to have a fit.

His lips pressed to my stomach just as it let out a low growl.

Ormiez chuckled. "Perfect timing. I asked Lirhop to start dinner before I went to meet with The Council. It should be ready now. Let's go feed the beast."

He planted another quick kiss on my belly and stood up, taking my hand in his.

"Wait." I pulled back to keep him in place. The garden was the perfect spot for me to show him. Ormiez loved it here. "I need to expel some of my power."

"Now?" He looked up at the second floor, where the kitchen was. "Can't we do it another time?"

"No. It's gotten to be too much strain on my body. Red will be here soon, and I need to be at full strength to deliver your enormous baby."

He laughed and kissed the back of my hand. "Okay. Do you need to sit down?"

"No, but close your eyes."

He did as I asked, and I allowed my power to flow from me and through him. Each time was like being reborn. My skin felt new after, my muscles stronger. As the weight of my power escaped into the air in glimmering blue specks, they wrapped around the plants and encouraged them to grow.

"Now open them."

"Exia." He breathed my name like a prayer.

This was why I wanted to do this here. To give him this moment. He had been working so hard since we left Xeonere's planet, always trying to show that he'd learned and he had changed. I wanted to reward him, to show him that the gods had been watching, and they were pleased.

I wasn't sure if my message came across clearly until he looked around at all the blooming flowers and herbs, his labor of love, and tears gathered in his golden eyes.

"Do you like it?"

"It's beautiful."

He pulled me close and kissed me just as the pink moon appeared in the sky.

AFTERWORD

I'd love to hear what you thought of this book. Please consider leaving a review on Amazon and Goodreads. Hearing from you all puts the battery in my back to get more words written.

Join my newsletter to be updated on my book sales, releases, and freebies. You can also follow me on social media to see my life in between book releases.

www.sukaliabrown.com

instagram.com/Sukalia_Brown

ALSO BY SUKALIA BROWN

The King's Summit

(Orej Zans Book 1)

A woman makes a deadly deal for her mother's freedom, but to collect on that deal, she'll need to survive two months on an alien planet, where everything and everyone seems to be out to get her.

ABOUT THE AUTHOR

Sukalia is an avid reader of sci-fi and fantasy. She's always longed to see more people of color on the covers and read about them going on epic journeys. Her novels focus on beautiful, three-dimensional Black people who are finding their joy in a magical world.